THE KILLER TRIP

D.M. FOLEY

REMEMBER YOUR ROOTS PRESS

ISBN: 979-8-9876505-4-7 (Hardcover)
ISBN: 979-8-9876505-5-4 (Paperback)
ISBN: 979-8-9876505-6-1 (ebook)
Cover Design by: Dawns Designs

To C.P. and L.S.
Thanks for the years of friendship and
adventures! I hope you enjoy
this book and smile.

CONTENTS

PART ONE

Laney

"You find out who your real friends are when you're involved in a scandal."
~Elizabeth Taylor

CHAPTER ONE

WHAT DID I DO?

I couldn't believe I was sitting in the back of a police car. The handcuffs were so tight they were digging into my wrists. This was my first time being arrested. Not that I hadn't ever committed a minor crime. Like the time I drove Michael McDonald's car home from the bowling alley when I was only fourteen and didn't have a driver's license.

He was a guy who lived in my neighborhood and hung out with a bunch of us. We ranged in age from fourteen to twenty-one years old. He was eighteen. Someone had given him some alcohol, and he was way too drunk to drive. Everyone else had already left, not realizing his inebriation. Since I had hitched a ride there with him, I needed to figure out how to get us back home. They locked the bowling alley up for the night and there were no outside pay phones around. So I did the next most reasonable thing. I drove us both home. It wasn't far, maybe five miles tops. I parked his car in his driveway and unlocked his front door.

Michael refused to go in though because he wanted his keys. He was the type of guy to just go out for a drive to clear his head, so I couldn't give him his keys in good conscience. His solution was to follow me home as I walked the short distance between our houses. The incessant begging from him was annoying, but I didn't give in. Even when he followed me into my house. We argued in whispers so we didn't wake my parents and eventually; I won out. Michael walked home without his keys. The next day, he thanked me. My thoughts about it were no harm, no foul.

It's ironic, though, now that I give it thought that most of my potential criminal behavior occurred around motor vehicles. The other instance was when I kind of stole a car. I was sixteen and had taken a road trip with some friends to Clair, Canada. We met some guys that we hung out with for the week we were there. Of course, I thought this one guy was super cute. His name was Arnold. His smile was a little crooked, but his brown eyes glowed and drew me in. The other guys called him Arnie. I didn't really care what his name was. He had a sweet ride that just made him even more attractive to me. It was a black trans am with a red pin striping down the sides. Technically, he had given me permission to drive it.

"It's locked. The keys are in my pocket. If you can get in it, you can drive it."

Those were his exact words. I think he wanted me to remove the keys from his pocket. His way of getting some cheap thrill or something. I had other plans. So I just remember smiling at him.

"You're on."

What he didn't know about me was I went to a technical high school and was in the automotive shop. I knew fully that it was common for teenage guys to have a spare key hidden under the wheel well of their car. I found the key, unlocked the door, jumped in, relocked the door, and started it, all with him standing six feet away with his mouth agape. The look on his buddies' faces and the laughter of my friends just egged me on. I only took the car for a spin around the block. When I returned and parked it, I threw the spare key back at him.

"Thanks for letting me take it for a spin! It's a sweet ride."

"You are crazy! You just stole my car!"

"Yes, I am crazy. Actually, no, I didn't steal it. You said if I could get in it, I could take it for a ride. You are the idiot that hid your spare key in an obvious spot."

He must have liked crazy girls because he asked me to go out on a date the next night. We went out; he dropped me off at my friend's memere's house and I never heard from him again. My friends and I left the next day to go back to Connecticut. That was thirty years ago. I hadn't thought about him or that trip in a very long time.

So when I sat in the back of a police cruiser arrested for his murder that apparently occurred the night we went out, I was beyond shocked. I didn't know he was dead, let alone that someone killed him. What I knew, I didn't do it. I am not even sure how they knew about me to even have me as a suspect. A week, that is all I knew this kid for.

We had one date, and it really wasn't all that eventful. Except I punched him in the nose when he tried to get to second base. He was fine though, just a little bloody nose that he cleaned up with a rag from his back seat before driving me home. He had apologized for trying to go too far.

My first thought after they slapped the cuffs on me was, *could I have broken his nose somehow and could that have killed him?* There was no way in my mind that his injury was enough to kill him. My mind searched the memories of that week, and that last night as the blue and red lights flashed in the darkness as rain fell and pelted the roof of the police cruiser.

CHAPTER TWO

SUMMER 1988

My parents had given in to my pleading to let me go with LeeAnn and Cora Lynn to visit LeeAnn's memere in Canada for a week. The catch was my sister Susan. My parents told me I had to bring her along. I was sixteen, and she was fifteen. We were born almost a year apart. Everyone joked we were Irish twins. The thing was, we could pass as twins except I was a tomboy into sports and she wasn't. Playing sports meant getting sweaty, messing up her hair and makeup, and that was unacceptable for Susan.

Susan and I ran with different crowds, which is why it annoyed me she had to go with me on the trip. LeeAnn and Cora Lynn tolerated her on my behalf, but they were tomboys like me, so we knew this trip would have some challenges with her along for the ride. I didn't understand why she had even pushed to go with us. It wasn't as if we were close.

We fought most of the time because she got her way always. Susan got out of doing household chores by pretending to be sick. They diagnosed her with leukemia when she was ten. She had been in remission since the bone marrow transplant, but that didn't stop her from getting out of things she didn't want to do. That meant a lot of times I had to pick up the slack. So I wound up doing her chores while she was packing for the trip.

"Hey Laney, where are the suitcases Mom and Dad took to Atlantic City last year?"

"I don't know. Probably in the basement. If you feel well enough to pack, I am sure you can do your chores. I still need to pack myself and now, because I have to do your work on top of my own, it will take me longer."

"I can rest while I pack. It is less strenuous than mopping the floor."

"I don't even know why you want to go with us?"

"Isn't it obvious? One, why should you have all the fun? And two, without you home, they will force me to do all the chores."

"Yeah, right. Mom and Dad wouldn't force you to do anything."

"They would too! When you aren't home, they always make me do the dishes. My nails are becoming brittle from it! Just look."

Susan held up her nails to show me how bad they looked. To me, there was nothing wrong with them. During the school year, I spent most nights staying over at LeeAnn's house. Sports were my lifeblood, and they were to LeeAnn and Cora Lynn as well. We were all athletes, and we played three sports together. Cross-country was my favorite and what I was best at. LeeAnn was a basketball star and Cora Lynn rocked at softball. We all played on all three of our school's teams. That was how we all met during my freshman year last year.

Cora Lynn had just graduated, so this trip was supposed to be a last hurrah for the three amigos. We were inseparable at school, even though we were in different grades and shops. Everyone knew we were like sisters. LeeAnn lived right across the street from the school, so with our practice schedules and games, it had been easier to stay at her house during the week. My parents didn't mind, it made it easier for them to have me stay there. They didn't have to drive to pick me up from practices or games.

It was an escape for me from the arguments my parents had constantly. Usually about money issues stemming from the medical bills from when Susan had been sick. Dad worked as much as one man could, but that was not enough for Mom. She needed things. In order to keep up with the other women in the neighborhood, she had to have the latest hairstyle, the latest fashion, and the latest home furnishings. Susan was a carbon copy of our mother's personality and I was our father's.

Susan trudged downstairs into the basement and was back in the kitchen where I was mopping within minutes.

"I found them both. They are on the top shelf in the laundry area. Can you go grab them?"

"Susie, I am busy. Remember, I am doing your chores!"

"They are too heavy for me to get down from way up there. You know how weak my body is. Do I need to tell Mom you won't help me? You are going to use one anyway, so why can't you get them down for us both?"

She had a point, so I begrudgingly put the mop into the bucket, haphazardly splashing water as I did. Susan shrieked and jumped back so none of the dirty mop water got on her. I went to the basement and grabbed the two suitcases. They weren't heavy at all. When I brought them upstairs, I brought one to Susan's room and one to mine and then got back to finishing the chores.

I had an hour to pack everything I needed for the week after I finished my work. As I entered my room, I saw the suitcase missing. When I went to Susan's room, she had both suitcases packed full of her things..

"Hey, one of those was for me to use."

"Well, I needed two. You are going to have to figure out something else."

I stomped back to my room and slammed my door shut. *Maybe I could lose Susan somewhere on the trip. No, then Mom and Dad would never forgive me.* In my closet, I found a big duffle bag that I had used the summer before for cross-country camp. It would have to do. I didn't have time to look for anything else. Cora Lynn and LeeAnn would be at our house in a half hour to pick us up and head on our way. I rolled up my outfits and placed them inside the duffle bag. Then I added a couple of pairs of flip-flops and sneakers. I packed for any weather.

A horn honked out in the driveway. Susan and I said our goodbyes to our mom and dad. We had to rearrange Cora Lynn's trunk to fit both of Susan's suitcases and my duffle bag, and then we were on our way.

CHAPTER THREE

THE INTERROGATION

The wipers on the patrol car's windshield moved back and forth with the swish-swish sound as the police officer drove me back to the police station. It was lulling me into a sense of living in a dream. This was all too surreal. Only two evenings before, I was tucking my kids into bed when LeeAnn called. Her voice was strained on the other end of the phone and I could tell she was holding back the tears. She had called to tell me of her memere's passing. I hadn't seen her grandma since her own wedding twenty years ago, but she wanted to know if I would attend the funeral with her. Cora Lynn would attend as well. It would be like our road trip thirty years ago, minus Susan.

We haven't spoken to Susan since she graduated high school. Her graduation party was all that she wanted, and she got it. Just like everything else in her life. The year before, after my graduation, our parents had said they couldn't afford a big party. I was okay with it. We had a few of my friends over for a backyard picnic and it was great. But that wouldn't do for Susan. She needed to be the center of attention. The party couldn't be in the backyard. That wasn't glamorous enough. So our parents rented the Moose Lodge hall. That was almost not good enough until Mom and Dad sprang for catering and a DJ.

It was at the party that we last spoke after I caught her making out with my boyfriend. It crushed me to see them together. Troy and I had been dating for almost three years. Coincidently, we met shortly after I got home from that trip we took in the summer of 1988. I made a big scene ruining her party, and dumping him. Went home, packed everything I could, and moved out of my house. I lived with LeeAnn for a while until I met Scott. Scott and I had been married for over twenty years.

The cruiser pulled into the station. When the officer opened the door, it interrupted my thoughts.

"I am taking you to booking and then we will bring you to the interrogation room."

I just nodded my head and let him lead the way. This all had to be some weird misunderstanding. The officer took my picture from the front and side. Then he took my fingerprints. When he completed the task, he led me down the hall into an interrogation room, where I sat at a table waiting. The door opened and two men in plain clothes with badges attached to their belts came in and sat down across from me. One had a file folder that he opened and started flipping through. The other spoke.

"My name is Detective Banks, and this is Detective Rodgers. We are going to ask you some questions."

I looked him in the eyes and just nodded. What else could I say or do? I still couldn't believe I was sitting here.

"Mrs. Wilson, you understand why you are here, right?"

"Yes, sir. The officer read me my rights and told me what I was being arrested for."

"Did you know Arnold Paltro?"

"I met a guy named Arnold thirty years ago. I don't know what his last name was. We only knew each other for a week."

"Did you go on a date with him?"

"Yes, the night before we were leaving to go home."

"Can you tell us what happened that night?"

"Sure. Arnold came by LeeAnn's Memere's house around 6 pm. He drove us to a local pizza joint. We had a fun time just talking and hanging out."

"Is that the only place you went?"

I could feel my cheeks blushing. Telling these two men about my teenage romance was em-barrassing. I didn't want to tell them about what else happened, but I knew I had to be honest if I wanted to clear myself.

"No, we crossed the border into Fort Kent and went to a Violette Settlement Road. Up by LeeAnn's uncle's cabin."

One detective looked at the other with a side glance and a raised eyebrow. This made me nervous.

"Go on. Then what did you do?"

"Well, Arnold parked the car. We started talking at first and then he kissed me."

I could feel my cheeks getting redder by the minute. Remembering that kiss. Arnold wasn't a terrible kisser. I actually enjoyed the kiss.

"What did you do when he kissed you?"

"Well, I kissed him back. We made out for a few minutes before he attempted to get further."

"What do you mean by getting further?"

They were going to make me say it. Seriously, I really didn't want to recount these details. I had all but forgotten about Arnie and our one date until they arrested me.

"Sir, I am sure you understand my meaning. But, if you need me to spell it out for you. He tried to get in my pants."

"What did you do when he did that?"

"I punched him in the nose."

Another side glance from the detectives. I was sure I was giving them more ammunition against me, but it was the truth. It would set me free. At least that was what I always thought about truth and honesty. I had watched enough crime dramas to know. It was always best to cooperate with the authorities.

"How did he react?"

"He yelled a bunch of explicative words, then grabbed a rag out of his back seat to stop the bleeding."

More side-eyeing. The detectives were giving me a guilty complex. The punch didn't kill him; he drove me home.

"Did he hit you back?"

"No. He drove me back to LeeAnn's grand-mother's house. That was the last time I saw him."

The detectives looked at one another. The one with the file shuffled through and pulled out some pictures. He placed three black and white grainy photos in front of me. There was Arnold's sweet Trans Am, with him in the driver's seat, and me in the passenger seat in the first picture. The second picture was the same except, you could see on our faces we were not as happy as before. The third picture was different. It showed my ball cap pulled down and my face wasn't showing as much. Just my chin. I looked at the pictures. They were me. Detective Banks must have noticed my facial expression because he started with more questions.

"Do you recognize these pictures?"

"I have never seen the pictures before, but I recognize Arnold's car and us in it."

"So you admit it is you in all three pictures?"

"Well, the first two are definitely me. The last one looks like my ball cap, but I can't see my face, so I can't say for sure it is me."

"But you admit it is your ball cap?"

"It looks like mine, but it was a generic white cap. Any girl could have the same cap."

"Were you wearing your ball cap the night you went out with Arnold?"

"Yes, I wore my ball cap, but it shouldn't be covering my face. I had my ponytail through the back. That's how I always wore it."

"Mrs. Wilson, they took the first picture at the border crossing at 7:30 pm. They took the second at 8:45 pm when you crossed back. Then the third, when you crossed back into Maine again."

"Sir, the third picture can't be me then. Arnold dropped me off at Memere's house right before 9 pm. That was my curfew."

"We have a witness that saw you climb out a window at 9:10. Perhaps to meet back up with Arnold, which would explain the third picture."

"Sir, I assure you. I didn't sneak back out to see him, or anyone else for that matter."

"What did you do when you got back then?"

"Well. Memere was waiting to make sure I made curfew. I said goodnight, then I got into my pajamas and went to tell my friends how my date went."

"What are your friend's names? We will need to talk to them."

"LeeAnn and Cora Lynn, they are staying at LeeAnn's Memere's house."

"The same house you stayed in before?"

"Yes."

A knock on the door interrupted the questions. Detective Rodgers got up and answered the door. Another officer handed him a piece of paper. Detective Rodgers closed the door and sat back down.

"Interestingly, your fingerprints match the ones found in the victim's car."

"Um, of course. I admitted I was in the car. That doesn't prove I killed anyone. I don't know what your witness saw, but it wasn't me. My friends and I stayed up talking until past midnight."

"We will talk to your friends. In the meantime, would you be willing to submit to a DNA test? You can do it willingly or we can get a warrant."

"What do you need my DNA for?"

"Well, there was blood from someone else at the crime scene. If it's not yours, then there is a possibility we can set you free."

If they were talking about the rag Arnold used to clean his bloody nose, then they possibly had evidence against me. If that was the case, then I had no hope. When I punched him, my ring cut into my finger. I used the rag to wipe the blood.

"Sir, you can take my DNA. I will give it willingly. But I must confess, I cut my finger with my ring when I punched him. I wiped it on the same rag he used to wipe the bloody nose."

Detective Banks left the room and came back with a DNA collection kit. He swabbed my cheeks. Then he left the room. When he came back, his demeanor changed.

"Mrs. Wilson, I am going to be straight with you. You might as well confess to killing Arnold. Your words have put you at the scene of the crime. We know you liked Arnold's car. In fact, we believe that was the motive for killing him."

"Wait a minute, you think I would kill a guy for his car? That's crazy!"

Detective Rodgers looked over the file in front of him and flipped through some pages until he found what he was looking for.

"No, Mrs. Wilson. You are crazy. Isn't that what you told Arnold in front of his friends when you stole his car the first time?"

They knew about my joyride. I was tiring of their questioning. They would never believe I was innocent. This was looking worse by the minute. Even I could see how everything pointed to me.

"Look, I didn't steal his car. He said if I could get in it, I could drive it. I got in it, without breaking into it, and I drove it around the block. I returned it. That's not stealing, that's borrowing."

"You stole it the night you killed him, though. You drove it an hour away and ditched it on the highway. Then you hitchhiked your way back. The trucker who picked you up gave a statement that he dropped you off at your friend's grandmother's house. That is two witnesses that saw you, before and after the murder."

"Why didn't you arrest me before if you knew I killed him?"

"We didn't have your name. Your friend's grandmother suffered a stroke the day after you all left. Her memory and speech were affected. No one knew who you were until you came back. We had received an anonymous tip that the girl who had gone on a date with Arnold would be back in town. Also, the bartender at the bar you and your friends stopped at the other night was a friend of Arnold's. He recognized you. I guess you never forget the face of the girl who killed your best friend. We contacted the border crossing. They had scanned your passports, so we finally had a name and face."

"I didn't kill anyone!"

"We will let the courts decide that. Contact a lawyer."

CHAPTER FOUR

1988

ROAD TRIP DAY 1

We hadn't been on the road for more than an hour when Susan needed us to stop. I swear her bladder couldn't hold much because she had gone before we left. Then she insisted we get food, but it couldn't be fast food. She was on one of the fad diets she had read about in *Teen Beat* or some other magazine she had read. I was already wishing my parents hadn't made us take her with us.

I don't remember the place we stopped at. What I remember was the waiter who waited on us. He was cute and roughly about nineteen. I could tell Susan had the hots for him by the way she was flipping her hair and flirting with him.

She wasn't happy when I slipped and told him her age.

"The children's menu is for fifteen and under, right? Susie, you should order from that."

LeeAnn and Cora Lynn snickered as Susan turned beet red. Then came the whining.

"The children's menu is for twelve and under, Laney. You know that. Stop being so mean to me."

The waiter rolled his eyes and tapped his pen on his order pad.

"Are you all ready to order, or do you need a few more minutes?"

We all ordered burgers and fries, except Susan, who ordered a salad with no dressing. I teased her she was going to turn into a rabbit instead of a supermodel. I actually got a chuckle out of the waiter with that one. Of course, it just soured Susan's mood even more.

The food was good and when we had finished; we made sure Susan used the bathroom before we got back on the road. While she was in there, the waiter came and gave us our check. He also handed me a slip of paper. It had his phone number and his name, with a brief note that said, "Call me."

It wasn't until we got in the car that I thanked Susan.

"Hey, thanks Susie, if we hadn't had to stop, I wouldn't have gotten that waiter's name and number. He was kind of cute."

"Are you kidding me? When did he give you his number? You are just messing with me because, you know, I thought he was cute. Just like you thought you were being slick with mentioning my age. And stop calling me Susie. That's a kid's name. My name is Susan."

I held out the piece of paper to show her I wasn't lying. Her eyes widened and her face filled with rage.

"Sure Susan, but thanks for also mentioning my name because, as you see, he remembered it and addressed the note to me."

She folded her arms and stared out the window as we headed on our way. LeeAnn turned up the radio and the rest of us sang along to every song that came on while Susan continued pouting. It was late when we finally reached the border of Maine and Canada. We all had our birth certificates to show we were U.S. Citizens, and we had to fill out paperwork where we were heading into Canada. The guards did a quick search of our car and then we were on our way to memere's house.

LeeAnn's grandmother was such a gracious woman. She welcomed us into her home with outstretched arms and lots of hugs. There were two guest rooms. One with two twin-sized beds and another with a queen-sized bed.

"Susan and I will take the queen-size bed, so you two can have separate beds. We are sisters. We can share a bed for a week."

"Absolutely not! I don't want to share a bed with you! It's bad enough I will have to share a room with you."

"Susan, stop being rude. We have to share a room. Memere's house isn't big. She has been gracious to allow us to come for a visit. Don't be a spoiled brat."

"Laney, Cora Lynn and I will share the queen-size bed. Then Susan can at least have her own bed, even if she has to share the room with you. Is that agreeable to you, Susan?"

LeeAnn was trying to smooth the tension like she always did. She pleaded with me with her eyes to give my sister a break.

"Thanks, LeeAnn, for understanding. I wish you were my sister and not Laney."

Susan stomped down the hallway to the bedroom with the twin beds, dragging both her suitcases with her.

"Memere, I am sorry for my sister's behavior."

"It is okay, dear. She is just used to getting her way. I can see that. Maybe a week here will help her. I expect you all to pull your weight while you are here. I am an old lady and taking care of four teenage girls is going to be a little more than I am used to."

"We will all help. We appreciate the opportunity to come to visit! If my sister doesn't do her share, I will pick up her slack, as I do at home."

"Oh, absolutely not. She will do her share under my roof. For now, though, you girls should settle in and get some sleep. You had a long trip."

We listened to memere and unpacked and went to bed. Susan insisted on sleeping in the bed closest to the window. I was tired of dealing with her already and just gave in to her wishes. I didn't really care where I slept.

The next morning, memere was in the kitchen making us breakfast. It all smelled so delicious. Three of us piled our plates with all the freshly made foods. Susan just ate a grapefruit and orange juice.

When we finished eating, Cora Lynn, LeeAnn, and I started clearing the table. Susan just sat there.

"Susan, I expect everyone to help with the cleanup here in my home after meals. So please come over to the sink and dry the dishes after I wash and rinse them."

"I don't feel very well. Can I please go rest instead?"

"Are you running a fever?"

"No, I don't think so,"

"Do you feel you are going to get sick?"

"No, I just feel tired."

"Well then, girl, you can rest after you dry the dishes."

The look on Susan's face was one of mortification. She begrudgingly picked up the dish towel and dried the dishes. We took turns taking showers after we completed helping to clean up after breakfast. I made my bed and left Susan in the room to finish getting ready for the day.

We left memere's house to go explore and wound up at a local pizza place. It had a small arcade. I started playing one of my favorite pinball machines. That was when the three guys came in. Susan started with her hair flipping and over-the-top flirting. The game engrossed me too much for me to really care about anything else.

When I got the top score, the guys came over. They were watching me. That was when I really noticed them. Especially the boy with dark hair and brown eyes.

"You are pretty good at this game."

"Thanks. I play it all the time at the bowling alley down home."

"Down home? Where are you from?"

"Connecticut. We are here visiting my friend's memere."

"Oh. What is your name? Mine is Arnold. These are my friends Steve and Maxwell. They call me Arnie."

"Nice to meet you, Arnie. My name is Laney. My friend over there with the long blonde hair is LeeAnn and the one with the short blonde hair is Cora Lynn. The one that looks like the Barbie version of me is my sister, Susan."

Arnold laughed.

"Is she your twin sister?"

"Nah, she is my Irish twin. We are born a year apart from one another."

I finished my game because Arnold was a bit distracting. We all sat together and ordered some pizzas. Except for Susan, she ate more salad. It shocked the guys when I ate a whole large pizza by myself.

"Where did you put all that?"

"I have a really high metabolism. I can eat what-ever I want and as much as I want and I burn off the calories quickly."

"Yeah, she got the lucky genes. I eat healthy and small quantities and have trouble with my weight. Not that I am overweight, but if I ate like my sister, I would be."

Susan tried to make herself sound like some sort of victim. I refrained from saying what I really wanted to say. That she was lazy and if she moved more and did more, she would burn more calories and could eat like me. You could tell the boys really didn't care what Susan had to say.

Steve was busy engaging LeeAnn in a private conversation, and Maxwell was trying to get to know Cora Lynn. Anytime Arnold tried to engage me in a conversation, Susan interjected herself into it.

We spent several hours hanging out and play-ing more arcade games with the guys, and then it was time for us to head back to memere's house.

When we said goodbye, they were quick to ask us to cross the border the next day to watch a Fourth of July parade. We agreed to go.

CHAPTER FIVE

INTERVIEW WITH LEEANN

Cora Lynn and I came down to the police station as soon as memere's funeral service was over. I still can't believe the police arrested Laney right there in the cemetery. This had to be some kind of misunderstanding. Laney was one of the kindest women I knew. Yeah, she was also tough and stood her ground, but murder, no way.

As they escorted us into separate rooms to be questioned, we briefly got a glimpse of Laney being led to a detention cell. She looked oddly calm about the situation. That was Laney, though. She kept her cool under the most stressful of circumstances. That was why I wanted her with me for my grandmother's funeral. I knew her calmness would help to keep me balanced.

Two plain clothes officers entered the room I was in.

"Mrs. Simpson, my name is Detective Banks, and this is my partner Detective Rodgers. Thank you for coming in. We would like to ask you some questions about your friend Laney Wilson."

"We came down to clear her name and get her out of here. So ask away."

"How long have you known Mrs. Wilson?"

"Sir, we have known each other for over thirty years. We met in high school and have been best friends since. More like sisters, actually."

"This isn't the first time you have traveled to Canada together, is that correct?"

"Yes, we came here together to visit my memere thirty years ago. We stayed for a week."

"That was when you all met Arnold Paltro and his friends, correct?"

"Was that his last name? We got none of the boy's last names. We didn't give them ours either."

"Yes, that has hindered our investigation over the years, that and your grandma having a stroke and having memory issues. She didn't know who had visited her or if you all were related to her. Because of her condition, we couldn't press her further for information."

"Well, I thank you for that. The last few decades after that stroke were difficult for her."

"You are welcome. What did Laney do the night of her date with Arnold?"

"What do you mean?"

"Walk me through that evening. From her getting ready to when she got home."

"Okay. Laney did little to prepare for her date. She wasn't one to wear make-up or do her hair fancy. If I remember correctly, she had put her hair in a ponytail and wore her white ball cap. When Arnold picked her up, he came to the door. Memere reminded Laney her curfew was nine o'clock, and they were on their merry little way."

"Was she back for her curfew?"

"Absolutely! Laney hated to be late for any-thing. She also didn't want to upset Memere. She loved and respected my grandmother."

"So she was home before 9 pm? What did she do when she got home?"

"She talked with Memere for a few minutes, then she went into her bedroom to get her paja-mas."

"Hold on, she wasn't staying in the same room as you?"

"No, she was sharing a room with Susan. But Susan was already asleep, so Laney grabbed her pajamas and came into our room to give us a rundown of the date."

"Who is Susan?"

"That would be Laney's little sister."

"So Susan was sleeping when Laney got home?"

"As far as we know, yes. Laney had put her pajamas on her bed before she left, so if Susan was asleep, she wouldn't wake her. She never turned the light on."

"What time did Laney stay in your room till?"

"She never left our room. We all fell asleep after midnight."

"What was Laney's impression of the date?"

"Well, it disappointed her that Arnold turned out to be a hound dog."

"A hound dog? I have never heard that before."

"It was our term for guys who just wanted to have sex."

"How did Laney feel about Arnold only wanting sex from her?"

"She was upset. Her hand hurt from punching him, but her heart hurt because she had finally thought she had met a guy who was different. She thought he liked her for who she was."

"Was she angry?"

"No, she was sad. She cried a lot as we talked through it all."

"So Laney never had sex with Arnold that night?"

"No. Laney was a virgin. She hadn't had sex with anyone. She didn't want to have sex while she was in high school."

"What about you and Cora Lynn? Were you also virgins?"

"Actually, yes we were."

"One last question. You said Laney was your best friend and, like a sister, would you lie for her?"

"No, sir. I love her. But I wouldn't lie for her."

"Can I ask you to stay here for a few days? We may need to ask you more questions."

"Sure, if it will help free, Laney."

The detectives left the room. Before they did, they said I could wait for Cora Lynn out in the lobby. Laney was being detained indefinitely. Since the actual crime occurred in Maine, she would have to be extradited to be arraigned. I couldn't understand why they asked if Cora Lynn and I were also virgins. What did our sexual status have anything to do with the murder case?

I went into the lobby and waited for Cora Lynn to be interviewed.

CHAPTER SIX

1988

ROAD TRIP DAY 2

The morning of our second day went better than the first morning. Susan seemed to understand that she needed to do things for herself around here. She even helped clean after breakfast without being asked. She still had to be reminded about making her bed, but it was a start.

We had a busy day ahead of us, and the sun was glowing. The boys would wait for us at the border so we could follow them to the parade. Susan was busy primping and preening herself.

"Come on Susan, we are going to be late to meet up with the boys. Just put your hair up in a ponytail like me and forget the make-up. Go for the natural look."

"Ugh, why would I do that? I don't want to look like you. You're bland."

"Really? If I am a more sterile version of you, then why do I get more attention from guys without even trying?"

I must have hit a nerve because she closed the bathroom door in my face. We were all ready and waiting for Susan. Thankfully, she only took a little longer. When she emerged from the bathroom, it surprised me to see her hair up in a ponytail like mine. Minus the ball cap. She still had a ton of makeup on, which was visible with the line between her chin and neck. The foundation she used was not her natural shade.

We met the boys at the border with five minutes to spare and followed them to the parade route. The town blocked the main street off because it was the way the parade participants would march, and the boys led us down several side streets to where we needed to park.

"You girls are going to love the vantage point of where we are going to watch from."

Maxwell excitedly led the way, holding Cora Lynn's hand. It was about a block away from where we parked and you could see the sides of the main street had throngs of onlookers packing both sides. We were coming up on a corner building and he veered right into a back alley. When he climbed the fire escape that led to the roof of the building, my stomach did a flip.

Heights were not my favorite thing, and it looked as though the best vantage point was from the roof of the building we were standing next to. I sucked in a breath as, one by one, we climbed up the fire escape. It was difficult trying to hide my fear in front of everyone. Thankfully, Susan didn't hide hers and put on quite the show. Her whining started the moment Maxwell showed we would climb to the roof.

"Why can't we watch the stupid parade from the street level?"

"Did you see the number of people along the route? We won't see anything."

"I don't care! It is too high to go to the roof. What if we fall off?"

"We will not fall off. Stay away from the edge if it scares you. But come on, we don't want to miss the parade."

It wasn't until the rest of us were almost at the top that Susan stomped her foot and climbed up after us. As Arnold held his hand out to me to help me over the ledge of the roof, I looked down at her. Her crying smudged her makeup. I almost felt sorry for her. When she reached the top, I helped her over the ledge. That was when she tried to nudge me off. I caught myself and looked at her with a scowl.

"What was that for?"

"I lost my balance. Oops."

"Oops? You tried to push me off a roof, Susan. That isn't an oops."

"Why would I do that on purpose? Do you really think that little of me?"

Everyone was staring at us both, so I shrugged it off and followed the guys to the front edge of the building. They were right. The view was amazing. I would not let my sister ruin my day. She knew I had a fear of heights as well, so I was sure she was trying to rattle my cage. As the parade started, my nerves settled. It wasn't a huge parade, but it was fun to watch, anyway.

When it was time to climb back down, the butterflies returned to my stomach. Susan insisted on going down first after Maxwell. I wound up being the last one off the roof. LeeAnn told us about her uncle's cabin down on Violette Settlement Road, close to where we were, so we went to check it out.

The boys followed us down a long dirt road. There were very few houses along the way and they were back from the road. Her uncle's property was at the end of the road. The cabin was all locked up since they used it during hunting season. On the walk back to the cars, I went to step on a log and saw a snake. I screamed and ran over to Arnold's car and jumped on the hood. Susan seized on the opportunity to make me look bad.

"What did you see, a mouse?"

"No, I almost stepped on a snake. It looked like a rattler!"

Arnold looked around over by the log sheepishly and his shoulders shuddered.

"Ugh, I hate snakes too! I don't blame you for freaking out. I would have done the same thing."

Susan rolled her eyes and pouted. She thought she would make me look bad and instead; she pointed out that Arnold and I had a fear of snakes in common. The more I hung out with Arnold, the more I liked him. He helped me off the hood of his car and checked for any dents.

We all crossed back over the border and went to the pizza place we had met them at the day before. Arnold insisted I try poutine. This was French fries and cheese curds topped with gravy. It didn't look appetizing to me at all, but he held out a bite full on his fork and I caved in and ate it. It was good. Susan just glared at me from across the table. The next day, the guys wanted us to join them for a fireworks display over the border. We agreed to meet up with them again and then we went home to memere's house.

I was getting into my pajamas when Susan confronted me.

"Why do you always get the guys liking you?"

"The guys don't always like me. Maybe it's because I act like I don't care if they do or they don't. You try too hard, and it is obvious."

"I don't try too hard. The magazines say guys like girls who take care of themselves."

"I take care of myself. Just differently. I exercise and I like to have fun and laugh. I don't need to put a bunch of chemicals on my face or in my hair."

"So you are saying boys like the bland instead of the dolled up?"

"Yes."

"I don't think they do."

"Okay, don't listen to me. I don't care, but don't keep whining that guys like me better than you."

INTERVIEW WITH CORA LYNN

I waited patiently for the detectives to come into the room to question me. They said they were going to talk to LeeAnn first. When they came in, they sat down across from me and introduced themselves.

"Mrs. Lockland, thank you for coming in to answer our questions. We appreciate it."

"No problem. I want to help clear Laney. I know she didn't kill anyone. It is totally against her personality."

"Well, I am sure that is what you believe. However, evidence shows us otherwise."

"What evidence?"

"We have two eyewitness accounts placing Laney outside the house during the time frame she committed the murder. We have fingerprints, and more than likely her DNA."

"Okay, so what questions do you have for me?"

"Did Laney steal Arnold's car in front of you?"

I laughed, remembering how Laney had used his spare key to get into his car and take it around the block.

"She didn't steal it. She borrowed it and took it for a spin around the block. He said she could if she got inside it. She did, without breaking in, I might add."

"Was she fascinated with his car?"

"She said it was sweet, but she said that about a lot of cars. We went to a technical high school. She was in the automotive shop. So it was her thing to know and like cars."

"Do you think she liked Arnold's enough to kill him for it?"

"No way! She already had a much sweeter project car that she was building back home. She had no need for his car. Plus, how would she get it home? If you think that would be a motive for her to kill, you don't know Laney."

"What would be a motive for her to kill someone?"

"Honestly, the only thing I could think of would be self-defense."

"So you think she killed Arnold because she was defending herself?"

"NO, she didn't kill Arnold. She gave him a bloody nose, but she didn't kill him."

There was a knock on the door that interrupted their questioning. Another officer brought some papers to the detectives. They looked over the information presented to them. Both raised their eyebrows and looked at each other. It was Detective Rodgers that spoke.

"Your friend's DNA matches to DNA found at the scene of the murder, and her DNA popped up at two other unsolved murder scenes. It seems as if your friend might be a serial killer."

"What? There is no way! I have known Laney for over thirty years."

"Did she know a Troy Hamel? Or a Daniel Eldridge?"

"She dated a Troy Hamel for several years until he cheated on her with her sister at her sister's graduation party."

"So she knew him? What about Daniel Eldridge?"

"Well, if it is the same Troy Hamel, then yes, but I don't believe she would have killed him, either. The Daniel guy doesn't sound familiar."

"What did she do when she found Troy was cheating on her?"

"She smacked him, broke up with him, and moved out of her house. She moved in with LeeAnn. I was living there too. As far as I know, she has never spoken to either of them since that day."

"Well, there is evidence linking her to all three murders. And from what we are seeing, there are several similarities between the crime scenes. I suggest you help her get a lawyer."

"I will help her pay for the best defense attorney we can find. There is no way she did this!"

"She is going to need it. She has a violent streak. Punching one of her victims prior to killing him and slapping another. That gives us motive and premeditation on at least two counts. The third, we will have to investigate further."

"Where was Daniel from?"

Detective Banks seemed annoyed with my question. However, I was trying to piece together everything that they had shared with me. Laney was not a murderer, especially not a serial killer. I wanted to help sow seeds of doubt in their mind. He looked through the information in front of him.

"Not that you need to know the information, but it might help jog your memory of how Laney knew him. He was from Massachusetts. He worked as a waiter at a local restaurant."

"When was he murdered?"

"They discovered his body on August 18th, 1988. The medical examiner concludes he was dead for at least a week."

"Laney could not have done that. She attended a three-week cross-country camp in Vermont the first three weeks of August that year. I drove her there and picked her up. I dropped her off the last weekend of July and picked her up on the third weekend in August. That was where she met Troy that summer and they started dating. She attended every summer through high school and college. Troy stopped going after they broke up. That was where she met her husband, Scott, the last year she attended."

"Where in Vermont was this camp?"

"They held it at Stowe, VT."

"So, how did you travel? The I91 corridor or the I95?"

"The I91 corridor sir, it was the fastest way there. We even visited Ben & Jerry's while we were there."

"So you didn't travel the I95 route at all?"

"That was the way we went to Canada at the beginning of July, but not the way we went to Vermont."

"Did you stop anywhere on your way to Canada?"

"Yes, we stopped because Susan needed to go to the bathroom and she was hungry."

"Where did you stop?"

"Some local restaurant."

It hit me as I was answering the detective's questions. The waiter gave Laney his number. I remembered how Laney threw away the piece of paper when we arrived at memere's house.

"Lazy Joe's?"

"Umm, it could have been. I really didn't pay attention."

"Did anything happen while you were there?"

"No, we got our food, ate, and left."

"Did you have a male or female server?"

"A male."

"Were there any negative interactions between him and Laney?"

"No, sir. Susan was flirting with him, and Laney was trying to dissuade him because she felt her sister was too young for him."

"And what did he do?"

"He gave Laney his name and number."

"What was his name?"

"Honestly, I never saw it. Laney showed Susan in the car and she was furious. When we got to LeeAnn's grandma's house, Laney threw the paper in the trash."

"She never contacted him?"

"No."

Detective Banks and Detective Rodgers gathered their notes and information and stood up. When they left, they told me I was free to go, but I should definitely work on getting my friend a lawyer. Hopefully, I planted those seeds of doubt. When I left and met back up with LeeAnn, the first thing we did was try to reach out to Scott, Laney's husband. Our phone calls went unanswered. We both left messages for him to call us ASAP and that it was an emergency concerning Laney.

CHAPTER EIGHT

1988

ROAD TRIP DAY 3

When we woke up on the third day of our vacation, we were all surprised to see Susan already dressed and helping memere to make breakfast. She had her hair up again in a ponytail and she had no make-up on. It was startling to see how much she looked like me without her usual face put on. Maybe this trip was a tipping point for my sister. Hopefully, the changes would stick with her when we got home. Except, I hoped she wouldn't take over my personality and copy me too much. I wanted her to find her true self.

"Good morning sleepy heads. Memere and I have been up and at em, while you lazy bones slept away."

"Good morning, Susan. Glad to see you finally pulling your weight without being told to. By the way, I like your new look."

"Laney, I always pull my weight. You just always treat me like a baby and that I can't do anything myself."

The audacity of Susan blaming me for her laziness. She knew she was lying. I could see the smirk on her face. If I made a scene here, it would just upset memere. I didn't want that. So I took the high road and changed the subject.

"What are we going to do today before we meet the boys for the fireworks?"

"Why don't we take Memere to the movies?"

LeeAnn hugged her grandma as she made the suggestion.

"That sounds like a great idea! It is the least we can do since she has been such a hospitable hostess."

Cora Lynn joined in the hug.

"A girl's day out! Sounds perfect!"

I joined in on the group hug. Susan sheepishly joined in as well and agreed a day with memere would be fun.

When we were all ready to head out we let memere sit up front with Cora Lynn. Susan complained about being squished in the middle of the backseat until I elbowed her and gave her a stern scowl. At the movie theatre, we got a big bucket of buttered popcorn to share and our drinks, then we settled down in our seats to watch *Short Circuit 2*. It was a funny movie and we all enjoyed it. We took memere out for a late lunch afterward. She appreciated the day out with all of us. It was late in the afternoon when we got home and we scrambled to change into some warmer clothes for our evening out with the boys.

I was wearing a Duke sweatshirt that I had gotten from a guy I worked with the summer before at the YMCA Day Camp. That was a fun summer. LeeAnn and I both worked there. We hung out with Chris and Greg, two other counselors a lot.

It was on one of the overnight sleepovers that Chris had given me his sweatshirt to wear because I had gotten cold. He was so sweet.

Susan walked out of the bedroom wearing a sweatshirt as well. Not a Duke one, but a dark blue. It was LeeAnn that noticed first.

"Whoa, I never realized how much you two look alike until right now. I guess with Susan always wearing her hair differently and wearing make-up, you couldn't see the similarities. But, now, holy moly, it is hard to tell!"

"Thanks, LeeAnn, I guess I never realized it as well. But looking exactly like my big sis might come in handy."

"Hey you might look like me, but you will never replace me. We have very different personalities."

"Challenge accepted."

I didn't like Susan's response. It gave me chills up my spine. *Was she trying to replace me?* The thought was preposterous.

The boys were waiting for us at the border. We followed behind them again as they led us to the park, where the fireworks would be set off. The place was packed with people and we all trudged through the maze of people to find a spot to put the blankets down to sit on. This was when Susan's personality came out, again.

"What? No lawn chairs? We have to sit in the grass on blankets?"

Her voice was so whiney and each of the boys rolled their eyes.

"Susie, you could have stayed at memere's, but you chose to tag along. Sitting on the blankets is fine. Get over it."

I grabbed Arnold's hand as I sat down on the blanket and he smiled sitting next to me. Susan's face turned beet red. She folded her arms and plopped awkwardly down on the other side of Arnold. He looked from side to side at us.

"Wow, I didn't realize how much you two looked alike until now. Susie, you are pretty like your sister without all that makeup. But maybe you should try to come up with your own look instead of copying hers."

Oof, that was going to sting. I almost felt a twang of jealousy when he first complimented her, but when he called her out for copying me, I knew that was going to piss her off. Susan immediately reached up to her ponytail and took the hair tie out. She shook her hair and ran her fingers through it. When she turned to him, she was smiling wryly.

"Is that better, Arnie?"

Then she leaned her head on his shoulder. His cheeks blushed. I didn't like the feelings that were bubbling up inside of me. We weren't an item, but I was feeling jealous of the attention Arnold was showing my sister. The first burst of light and bang of the fireworks made us all jump. Susan screamed like a little girl and I laughed. I leaned back on my elbows and tilted my head up toward the sky to watch the fireworks. The crowds oohed and ahhed. Some people clapped. Susan tried to cuddle up to Arnold, jumping with each bang. He shrugged her off of him and leaned back on his elbows.

"So are they better watching like this?"

"Of course! They are even better when you lie flat on your back. It looks like you are going through space. You know like the scenes in *Star Wars* when they are zooming through the universe?"

I fell back onto my back and he followed suit, tilting his head closer to mine.

"This is cool! I never even thought of watching them like this."

"You don't get neck strain either."

He laughed and as the next burst of light flashed, I caught Susan's fury as she watched us. I never saw her so angry. I couldn't understand what her problem was. It wasn't like Arnold and I were going to become a couple. Or she and Arnold would. We lived in different countries. This was just hanging out and having fun. I wished she would just learn to enjoy the moments in life instead of getting upset over everything. At that moment though, if looks could kill, I would be dead and so would Arnold.

CHAPTER NINE

THE PHONE CALL

I sat in my detention cell. It was cold and damp. The cot was hard. There was a sink with a faucet that kept dripping. It was getting annoyingly louder the longer I sat there. An officer came to the door of the cell.

"Mrs. Wilson, Detective Banks, and Detective Rodgers need to speak with you again. You are coming with me. Please turn around so I can cuff you."

"Okay,"

I complied with the officer and he brought me back to the interrogation room, where the two detectives were waiting for me.

"Mrs. Wilson, we hope that sitting in the detention cell has brought you to your senses and you are ready to cooperate."

"With all due respect, Detective Banks, I have been cooperating. I killed no one."

"Well, the evidence says otherwise. Your DNA matches the DNA found at the scene of the crime."

"I already told you it would, and why."

"Yes, you did. However, your DNA was linked to two other unsolved murders."

"What? What murders? I already told you, I never killed anyone. Who else did I supposedly murder?"

"Do the names Daniel Eldridge or Troy Hamel ring any bells?"

OMG, Troy. Troy was dead and someone murdered him? I hadn't seen him or heard about him since the day I found him lip-locked with my sister Susan. Troy was my first love. He broke my heart cheating on me, but I never wished death on him. I felt the sting of tears welling up.

"Troy was my first love. I didn't know he was dead, let alone that he was murdered. As for the other name, it doesn't ring a bell at all."

"We know about Troy cheating on you with your sister and you slapping him."

"Yeah, so? He broke my heart, I slapped him. That was all. I didn't kill him."

"Daniel was a waiter. The waiter that gave you his number on your trip to Canada."

"Oh, I didn't remember his name. He slipped me his name and number. I wasn't interested and threw the paper out when we got to Memere's house. That was the only time I saw him."

"They found your blood at all three crime scenes. How do you explain that?"

"I don't know. I explained what happened between me and Arnold. When did Troy and Daniel die?"

"Daniel died in August 1988, a month after Arnold. Troy died the summer of 1992."

"I was at a cross-country running camp in August 1988. As for Troy, I hadn't seen him since the summer of 1991."

"That is what your friend said. We suggested they get you a lawyer. The evidence is strong against you. We are moving to have you extradited to Maine since the first crime occurred there."

"Can I call my husband? I don't want him to worry about me."

"Sure. Here you can use this phone."

They slid a phone to me, and I raised my cuffed hands.

"Do you mind dialing it for me and holding the phone to my ear?"

Detective Rodgers dialed the number and held the receiver to my ear for me. The phone rang a few times and then Scott answered.

"Hello?"

"Scott, it's Laney. They have arrested me in Canada for a murder I didn't commit. Now they are saying they have evidence against me for two other murders. Troy Hamel and some other guy named Daniel. I am scared, Scott."

"Who is this? Is this some kind of game or scam? My wife is sitting right here next to me."

"Scott. It's me. Laney, your wife. What do you mean your wife is sitting next to you? I am still in Canada!"

"My wife came back the next day from Canada. LeeAnn? Cora Lynn? Haven't you hurt my wife enough? Is this one of your sick games?"

"Scott, I don't know what you are talking about. I didn't come home. I am in custody. They are talking about extradition! Call LeeAnn or Cora Lynn, they will tell you!"

My heart was racing. I felt as if I was in an episode of the *Twilight Zone*. My husband was acting as if he didn't know me. He thought I was home already. *Who was in my house with my family?*

"I don't know who you are, but you need to leave me alone."

The click of the phone hanging up on the other end, followed by silence, shattered my heart. My husband didn't believe it was me on the other end of the phone. The tears streamed freely down my face. Detective Rodgers hung up the phone for me when the conversation stopped.

"Mrs. Wilson, are you okay?"

"No, I don't understand what is happening. Please wake me up from this nightmare."

"What did your husband say to you to get you so upset?"

"He said I wasn't me. He said his wife was sitting next to him, and that she had returned from Canada the day after she had left, implying that LeeAnn and Cora Lynn had done something to me, her. I don't know what is happening. I am so confused."

"You are saying there is a woman at your house impersonating you?"

"I don't know. That is what it seems like."

"Mrs. Wilson, we are going to return you to your cell. Hopefully, your friends have found you a lawyer."

I just nodded my head. The officer came into the room and brought me to my cell. All of this was too much. My husband of over twenty years was home, thinking I was with him. *Who the heck could impersonate me?* Then it hit me like a ton of bricks, Susan!

Chapter Ten

1988

Road Trip Day Four

We got home late after the fireworks. Susan was quiet on the ride back to memere's while the rest of us laughed and talked about the boys. I tried not to let on how much I was falling for Arnold. It was crazy to fall for him. There was no way a long-distance relationship would work between two teenagers. He was cute, though.

My mind wandered to the memory of lying next to him, watching the fireworks and his head touching mine. It was a perfect night, except we weren't alone. If we had been, I just might have kissed him. The thought of that made my cheeks feel warm and butterflies fluttered in my belly. The next day, we were going to a lake with them.

I grabbed my pajamas and joined LeeAnn and Cora Lynn in their room. Susan slammed the door behind me. We stayed up late, giggling and swooning over Arnold, Steven, and Maxwell.

The next morning Susan was up early helping memere again. When we joined them, I noticed Susan was wearing her hair down, but still no make-up. She had her bathing suit on under her shirt and I could tell it was her pink bikini by the ties behind her neck. I was feeling self-conscious in my bikini. I didn't fill mine out nearly as well as she did hers. My athletic build didn't give me the curves she had, and that twinge of jealousy returned.

Memere packed us a lunch to take with us to the lake and we headed out to meet up with the boys. It wasn't very warm, and I wasn't sure I would even go in the water. Arnold was the first of the guys to take off his shirt and run into the water. He went under and came up shaking the water from his hair. With his crooked grin and his six-pack abs, it convinced me to join him in the cold water. I shimmied my cut-off jean shorts off but left my white t-shirt on.

I wasn't in a rush to go in the water. The minute my toes hit the coldness, I almost regretted my decision to join Arnold. Maxwell and Steven went splashing by me into the water and wrestled with Arnold. Their antics soaked me and I went further in the water to get acclimated. LeeAnn and Cora Lynn joined us while Susan stayed on the shore, but made herself known. As she shimmied out of her shorts and she took her shirt off, she flaunted her curves as she set herself up to sunbathe.

All three of the boys stopped and watched her. Until we ambushed them with some splashing. They turned and captured each of us, throwing us into the water.

"Hey, you gals up to going over to the rope swing?"

It was Maxwell asking and pointing over to a rock ledge with a rope. It wasn't too high, but it was high enough to make me more than a little queasy at the thought. I didn't want to look like a scaredy cat, so I agreed to go. We swam over and made our way up to the rock ledge. Maxwell was the first to go. It looked like fun. As everyone took their turn one by one, my nerves built. Before Arnold went, he looked at me and smiled.

"You don't have to do this if you don't want to."

"I want to, but it makes me nervous."

"Look, if it makes you feel better, I will wait for you in the water after I go."

"Thanks, that helps a little."

"No problem."

He held onto the rope and ran, swinging himself off the ledge. As he let go, he waved to me and plunged into the water. It made me laugh. The others were heading back up to the ledge and, as promised, he floated in the water, waiting for me.

I grabbed the rope and ran. As my feet left the ledge and I swung in the air, I felt a jolt of adrenaline. I let go and held my nose before hitting the water. I sank and then shot back up out of the water. Arnold swam over to me to make sure I was okay.

"That wasn't so bad, was it?"

"No, that was awesome!"

We took several more turns and then returned to shore to have lunch. Susan was still sunbathing.

"Perfect timing. Hey Arnold, can you please put some lotion on my back and shoulders?"

She was trying so hard to get his attention. It was really annoying. He shrugged his shoulders and rubbed the lotion on her back. She looked at me and stuck her tongue out. We all sat and ate. When we were done, we knew we needed to wait before we went back into the water. Steve stood up and threw a Nerf football to Maxwell. He caught it and threw it towards Arnold.

I jumped up and intercepted it and started running. Arnold tried to catch up, to no avail. I laughed and spiked the ball.

"I never saw a girl who could play football."

"Well, obviously, you never met me before now."

"You are so different from the girls up here."

"Really? What are the girls like up here?"

"They are more like your sister, Susan. You are pretty unique, you know that, Laney?"

"Well, thanks."

I was blushing, I could feel it in my cheeks. What else was I supposed to say? I wanted to kiss him right then and there, but everyone was there watching. Instead, I yelled to LeeAnn to go long and threw the football. When she caught the throw, I looked at Arnold and saw his mouth agape. Apparently, he had never seen a girl who could throw a football that far before.

We played more football and worked up quite a sweat. Before we went back into the water, I took off my T-shirt.

"Hey Laney, do you need help putting some suntan lotion on? I can help you if you want."

It shocked me that Arnold was actually offering to help me.

"Sure, thanks."

I caught Susan's look on her face as she watched Arnold help put the lotion on me. His touch brought butterflies to my belly and the warmth to my cheeks. I really wanted to kiss him now, but again, I resisted the urge.

As we entered back into the water, Susan joined us. She tried flirting with Arnold by splashing him. He seemed annoyed and responded with a pretty big splash back. He swam away from her and headed back to the rope swing. I chuckled, thinking Susan was probably not going to want to try it. She surprised me though when she took her turn. When she went under the water, I never expected her bikini top to come off.

She came up out of the water and covered the front of herself with her arms as her top floated nearby.

"Hey Arnold, can you be a gentleman and help me with my bikini top?"

He blushed and swam over to her with her top in his hand. When he handed it to her, she tried to cover herself, but then flashed him briefly while smiling. She turned around from him to put her top on and then swam back to the ledge.

When she was up on the ledge, I approached her.

"That was pretty slick of you to take your top off."

"It's not my fault. I actually have something to show."

As she walked past me, she nudged me, almost knocking me off balance. It wasn't until she did I realized how close to the edge of the ledge I was. That was the second time in as many days that she seemed to try to cause me to fall. If I didn't know any better, I would think my sister was trying to hurt me intentionally.

Chapter Eleven

Meeting with the Lawyer

I awoke in my detention cell. Every bone in my body ached along with my stiff muscles. It was probably the worst night's sleep in my entire life. As I slowly sat up, my eyes hurt from all the crying I had done the night before. The thought of losing Scott and my kids broke me. I still couldn't comprehend why he thought I was home. A female officer approached my cell.

"I am to take you so you can shower. There will be a change of clothes for you. Prison garb. Then your lawyer will meet with you."

"Okay."

The officer had to handcuff me to take me to where I would shower. She had to be in the room with me. When I was done, she placed me back in cuffs and led me to the interrogation room. There was a man in a crisp grey suit. He stood up when I entered the room.

"Hello Mrs. Wilson, my name is Attorney Peterson. Your friends hired me. They have filled me in on your predicament. Have a seat and we will chat, shall we?"

I had a seat across from him.

"Hi, it's nice to meet you. I hope you can get me out of here."

"I am going to try my best. First things first, I need to ask you a few questions. Is that okay?"

"Yes, I have been upfront and honest with the detectives. I will be truthful with you as well."

"Good. When was the last time you saw the victim Arnold alive?"

"When he dropped me off at Memere's house before 9 pm the night of our date."

"What did you do after he dropped you off?"

"I spoke to Memere, got my pajamas from my room, then went to LeeAnn and Cora Lynn's room to change and tell them about my date."

"Did you sneak out of the house through a window to meet back up with Arnold?"

"No, sir. I stayed up past midnight talking with LeeAnn and Cora Lynn until we fell asleep."

"So there was no way either of them could have snuck out of the house either?"

"No. We were together the whole time."

"Your sister was on the trip with you all as well, correct?"

"Yes."

"Do you know where I can get in touch with her to interview her?"

"Honestly, you would have to contact my parents. I haven't spoken to my sister since June 1991 at her graduation party. I caught her with my then boyfriend Troy."

"Did she have a habit of going after the boys you dated?"

"I dated a little in high school. There wasn't much time for that with sports and academics.

But, now that I think about it, yes, the guys I liked, she chased after them as well."

"You said you caught her with your ex-boyfriend, Troy. That is Troy Hamel, correct? One of the other boys they are claiming you murdered."

"Yes. I didn't kill him, or anyone else, for that matter. I hadn't seen him since the graduation party."

"Who else did your sister go after that you liked?"

"Well, Arnold. Every time he showed an interest in me the entire week, she tried to get his interest and attention."

"Where was she when you got home from your date?"

"In bed sleeping."

"Are you sure of that?"

"Well, I didn't turn the light on because I didn't want to wake her up. And it looked like she was in bed, or someone was. Again it was dark."

"So you don't know if she was actually in the bed or whether she was the one that climbed out the window?"

Omg, he was right! I didn't know for sure if Susan was asleep in bed. All these years, I had just assumed she was. But stating that would imply that my sister could have committed the murder. I may not talk to her anymore, but she was still my sister. Could I imply she was the murderer to save me?

"No. I don't, but I don't think my sister would have killed Arnold either."

"Look, my job is to defend you. If that means implying the plausibility that someone else could have committed the murder, even your sister, then so be it. I don't have to prove she did it. I just need to bring up enough doubt that it is possible that she could have committed the crime and not you."

"But what about the DNA evidence?"

"Yeah, I wish you would have waited and spoken to me first before consenting to that."

"Sorry, I was upfront and honest. I told them I cut myself with my ring when I punched Arthur."

"Yes, and that sounds plausible, which can sow doubt in a judge's or jury's mind. But, it doesn't help in the other two cases. Your blood was found there, too."

"That doesn't make any sense to me, though. For one thing, I was in Vermont at the time of Daniel's murder, so how could my blood get to the crime scene?"

"That is in your favor. You couldn't be in two places at once. Of course, I will have to verify your attendance at the camp you claimed to be at during that time."

"Of course."

"Is your sister a twin sister?"

"No. We are actually born a year apart. We were called Irish twins for that reason, and we looked remarkably alike. Why do you ask that?"

"Well, if you were actually identical twins, you would share DNA. It would be another way to sow seeds of doubt."

"Oh, okay."

"So Daniel was a waiter you met on the way to Canada, correct?"

"Yes. My sister was flirting with him, but he was way too old for her, so I tried to dissuade him from being interested in her. I embarrassed her and he thought it was funny. Then he gave me his name and number, but I never even called him. I threw the paper away when we got to Canada."

"Could your sister have grabbed the paper from the trash?"

"I suppose she could have."

"Okay, I am going to share this information with my team and my private investigator. We have some work to do to track down your sister and follow up on that summer camp. Please do not worry. I am confident we can successfully get you out of this mess."

"Can you get in touch with my husband and tell him I am really in jail? I called him yesterday, and he didn't believe me. He said his wife was sitting next to him on the couch."

"Sure thing Laney."

My attorney left the room, and an officer escorted me back to my cell. I didn't like the fact he was going to imply my sister did the killings instead of me, but if it was only to sow seeds of doubt and get me set free, I was okay with it. Not trusting my sister didn't mean I didn't love her. If I didn't love her, I wouldn't have offered to give her a bone marrow transplant for her leukemia when she was ten and I was eleven.

My parents didn't have to ask me. As soon as they said it was the best treatment to fight the cancer, I offered to get tested. When I was a match, it was a straightforward decision to help save her. Would she be willing to return the favor and help save me now?

CHAPTER TWELVE

1988

ROAD TRIP DAY FIVE

The weather forecast for the next day called for rain. We made plans to meet the guys for pizza and then the movies. When we got home from the lake, Susan was complaining of sunburn and soaked in the tub for an hour. It didn't really help because when she got out; she was still complaining. Memere told her to wet some towels and put them on the sunburn to draw the heat out. She did this for a while, but still complained. Finally, she fell asleep. I went to LeeAnn and Cora Lynn's room to sleep for the night. I didn't want to hear my sister complain all evening.

It was pouring when we got up the next morning. Susan wasn't out of bed. I checked on her and she was in tears crying over her sunburn. I felt bad for her and helped her get more towels to put on her. Memere said she would take care of her while we went out. Susan had protested, but Memere won out.

The three amigos were finally free of Susan for the day. We met the guys at the pizza shop. It was Maxwell that noticed Susan's absence first.

"Hey, where is your little shadow?"

"It seems she got a pretty bad sunburn on her back and shoulders."

"Oops, I guess I didn't do a good job of applying the sunscreen."

He nudged Maxwell, and they both laughed.

"I know she is annoying, but it's not funny that she is in pain."

"Sorry, I didn't mean to laugh at her being in pain. She just was getting on my nerves a lot. I'm not interested in her, and she is basically throwing herself at me."

"Yeah, I am sorry about that. I don't know where she gets that from. She seems to think that's what guys like."

"Well, this guy doesn't."

"Noted."

The rest of the time before the movie, we took turns playing pinball games. They still couldn't believe how good I was at them. Then we headed to the movies to see *Who Framed Roger Rabbit*.

Arnold sat next to me and we shared a big tub of popcorn. On more than one occasion, our hands touched when we both went for more. Each time it happened, I felt the urge to hold his hand, but I resisted. He smiled every time and slowly raised his hand and put the popcorn in his mouth. I still wanted to kiss him. This would be a perfect opportunity in a dark theatre. But I couldn't muster up the courage. He hadn't at-tempted to hold my hand or kiss me, so he must not have been interested. At least those were the thoughts running through my head at the time.

On more than one occasion, I looked over and saw LeeAnn kissing Steven and Cora Lynn kissing Maxwell. That just solidified in my mind that Arnold wasn't interested in me. I wasn't too worried. We only had two more days and then we would head home, anyway. There was no real reason for me to get involved with him, although I couldn't deny I liked him.

After the movie, we went to get some ice cream. It had finally stopped raining. Maxwell and Steven wanted to ride with Cora Lynn and LeeAnn, which meant I hopped in with Arnold. His Trans Am was a pleasant ride. I really wanted a chance to drive it, but I knew how most guys were with their vehicles, so I didn't bother asking. We got to the ice cream place, and all walked up to the window to order.

When we had all gotten what we wanted, we went and sat at some picnic tables. Arnold sat next to me and nodded over at his car.

"So, what do you think of my ride?"

"It's nice."

"Just nice? Do you know how many girls would die to ride in it? And you just did."

"A ride in a nice car isn't that big of a deal to me. Now, driving a nice car, that would be a big deal."

He stood up, pulled his keys out of his pocket, and then put them back in. Of course, I would not give him the cheap thrill he was looking for, but I was definitely going to get to drive his car the way I wanted to. The look of astonishment on his face as I drove away was one I would never forget. When I parked it and he had calmed down, he asked me out.

"Laney, you want to go on an actual date tomorrow night? Just you and me?"

"Do you forgive me for taking your car on a joy ride?"

"Of course I do. You are crazy, but I think I like crazy. I have had so much fun hanging out with you this week. Minus your annoying sister."

"Sure, it sounds fun, just you and I hanging out with no one else."

"It's a date then. We will figure out times tomorrow since we are playing baseball with you all in the morning, right?"

"Yeah, I am sure Susan will be there in the morning though too, just warning you."

"It's okay. I can handle a little time with her, knowing I will have you all to myself later."

Arnold followed Cora Lynn back to Memere's house, and Maxwell and Steven got back in his car when I hopped out.

PART TWO

SUSAN

"Deceiving others. That is what the world calls romance."
~ Oscar Wilde

CHAPTER THIRTEEN

COMING HOME

My parents slipped and told me Laney was going out of town. They rarely tell me much about my sister anymore. We haven't spoken to one another since my graduation party. She found me kissing her boyfriend, Troy. What she didn't know was I had revealed to him he had been dating the both of us, unbeknownst to him, the whole time. He thought it was her sneaking out of the house after curfew to have make-out sessions when it was me. Troy and I dated for a year after that incident. Then he disappeared from my life.

I have waited a long time to put my impression of her to the ultimate test. That time had come.

Laney was going to Canada, just as she had done thirty years ago. How poetic. That was where I learned I could pass myself off as her. Now it would set the stage for me to take over her life completely.

Scott was her husband of over twenty years. We never met. That was about to change. Laney hadn't even invited me to their wedding. My parents had pictures, though. Her husband was handsome, much better looking than her past escapades. No wonder she wanted to keep me away from him. I always knew Laney was insecure about herself and I used that to my advantage.

I had watched my sister from afar for years now. Her routine was predictable, so it would be easy to replicate. Even her looks would be easy to duplicate. She hadn't changed those in decades, either. Looking in the mirror, I smiled. I knew I could pass myself off as her. Now, to set the stage, I needed to make a few phone calls. First to our mother. It always annoyed me at how long it took her to answer the phone, even though I know her cell phone was never far from her hands.

"Hello Susan, I was just getting ready to go grocery shopping."

"Hi Mom, this won't take long. I just wanted to let you know I would be going out of the country on a business trip. My boss says it will be an extended trip. I didn't want you to worry if you didn't hear from me for a couple of days or weeks."

"Oh, you won't have phone service where you are going? Or postal service?"

"Mom, I will be working a lot. It is an extensive project. Long hours and such. You know the time difference will make it hard to connect. I will try to call once in a while."

"Oh, Okay. Well, Laney should be home in a few days, anyway. I wish you two were on speaking terms. It just breaks my heart knowing you two aren't as close as you used to be."

"That was Laney's choice, Mom, not mine. She is the one that can't forgive and forget. Not me."

"If I remember correctly, you had a hand in what happened."

"I was a teenager, Mom. I made a stupid mistake that she has made me pay for my entire adult life."

"Well, maybe when she gets back from her trip and you get back from yours, you two can work things out finally."

"Sure, Mom. If Laney wants that, I am certainly agreeable to it."

I lied, and I hung up the phone. Laney wasn't going to come back from her trip. Not if I had anything to say about it. The next phone call I made was to the Maine State Police. They were very interested in the information I had about a murder committed thirty years ago. Thankfully, I could give the information anonymously.

The day Laney left for Canada, I was watching. I needed to see the type of suitcase she had. It was a blue hardcover rolling one. Perfect. I knew where I could get one, just like it. After I purchased it, I packed it with Laney-type clothing. The bland and boring.

I patiently waited a day, and then I made a tearful phone call from the bus station.

"Hello?"

The voice on the other end sounded a little raspy, as if they were just waking up, but otherwise, it was pretty darn sexy.

"Scott, I need you to pick me up at the bus station in New London. LeeAnn and I had a falling out. I came home by myself on a bus."

"Oh honey, what happened? Why aren't you using your cell phone? Why didn't you call me to come to pick you up?"

"It's a long story, hun. Can I just tell you on the way home? I am exhausted. I need a new phone though and IDs, credit cards, and the works. In my rush to get out of there and away from them, I left my purse and everything in it."

"Dear, can't you just ask for your purse back when they come back? I am sure whatever this is about will smooth over. You are like sisters. You will work it all out."

That stung. Work it out like sisters. Laney hadn't spoken to me in decades. She didn't know how to work things out. I needed to make him understand.

"No, there is no working this out. I never want to speak with them again. Do you hear me? I don't want you talking to her either. Or Cora Lynn. They are just as dead to me as my actual sister, Susan."

"Okay, honey. I will be there soon. Love you."

"Thanks, love you too."

That was easy. Hook line and sinker. Now I just needed to wait for my handsome hubby to pick me up from the bus station. I didn't have to wait long before he came inside looking for me. Throwing my arms around him, I started the waterworks again.

"I am so glad to see you. Let's go home."

"Laney, honey, you are okay. I am here. Can you tell me exactly what happened? I have never seen you this upset."

"Scott, do I really have to recount all the horrible details right now? I just want to go home, soak in a nice relaxing tub, and go to bed next to you."

"Okay, but we need to stop at the phone store on our way home. You need a new phone and we need to stop at the bank to get you your new debit card and have the other one shut off."

"I guess we do, don't we?"

I shut off the tears and wiped my eyes. We walked together towards his truck. He put my suitcase in the backseat and then held the passenger door open for me. *Bless his heart, he was a gentleman.*

CHAPTER FOURTEEN

1988

ROAD TRIP DAY FIVE

I woke up still in pain from my sunburn. Laney had slept in LeeAnn and Cora Lynn's room again. I was fine with having the entire bedroom to myself. When they had gotten home from the movies, they were all excited because Arnold had asked Laney out on a date for tonight. She would not have the last say with him. I would make sure I got my shot at him, one way or another. Even if I had to pretend to be her to get it.

We were going to meet up with the boys after breakfast to play baseball with some of their friends. I planned on just watching. There was no ounce of desire for me to get all sweaty playing some dumb game. I would, however, enjoy watching the different guys play it. I couldn't understand how Arnold could find Laney attractive. It's not like she was pretty in any sense of the word. And she certainly didn't have any curves, like me, that one would think the guys would like.

I dressed like my sister again. This was extremely against my very being. Her style was that of Jo on *The Facts Of Life,* while mine was more like Blair's. She didn't seem to mind. It actually seemed to please her. I was imitating her. I felt so uncomfortable without my hair and make-up done just right. But if it meant a chance with Arnold, it was worth it.

As I entered the kitchen for breakfast, Memere was setting the rules down for Laney's date later in the evening.

"I don't mind you going on a date while you are here, but these are my rules. The boy comes in and meets me when he picks you up. And you are to be inside my house by 9 pm. Not outside in the driveway, making out. Inside by 9 pm. You understand?"

"Yes, Memere. I will let Arnold know this morning those are your conditions, and of course, I will follow them."

Laney is the rule follower. Well, I would not follow any rules except my own. I made sure I wrote Arnold a brief note from Laney. I would give it to him when we met up with him later.

We met up with Arnold, Steve, Maxwell, and some of their friends at the local high school ball field. I watched as they picked teams. Of course, Arnold picked Laney to be on his team. I rolled my eyes. Watching the two of them flirt back and forth made me sick to my stomach. The game dragged on, and I was extremely bored. It didn't help that my skin still hurt and now it was itching. When Laney scored the winning run, Arnold ran over to her and picked her up. Her feet swung in the air as he spun around. They were laughing when they came over to me.

"Susie, everyone wants to go get a bite to eat. You okay with that?"

"Sure, Laney. It's not like I have anywhere else to go."

So we headed to a burger joint down the road. I ordered a salad, which honestly I was tired of eating. As we all sat and ate, some freckle-faced kid sat next to me and slid his arm around the back of my chair. This was his attempt at flirting with me. I couldn't even remember his name if I tried. When Laney went to the bathroom, I handed Arnold the note and leaned close to his ear.

"My sister wanted me to give this to you. Don't show anyone or she will get in trouble."

"Okay. Thanks. I won't show or tell anyone."

When he opened it up and read it, his crooked little grin widened. Laney came back from the bathroom and sat next to him. They giggled amongst themselves quite a bit until everyone started leaving. We headed back to Memere's house so Laney could get washed up and ready for her date.

Six o'clock came and Arnold rang the doorbell. Memere let him in and grilled him for a couple of minutes before letting Laney go on her date. I went to bed early after dinner. Or that's what I told everyone else. I set my bed up to look like I was sleeping and waited patiently for Arnold to drop my sister off. When he did and he drove down the street, I climbed out the window. I ran down the street to the stop sign where Arnold was waiting in his car. I hopped in.

"Wow, I didn't think you were going to come back out after what happened."

Panic filled me. *What had happened?* I looked at his face and saw the swelling of his nose and some dried blood.

"I'm sorry. Are you okay?"

I hoped he would fill me in on what had occurred.

"Yeah, I am okay. I never had a girl punch me before. I don't know which is bruised more, my nose or my ego."

She punched him. Knowing Laney, he probably tried going further than she wanted to let him go.

"I am truly sorry. I just wasn't ready. You caught me off guard, I guess."

"So now you are?"

He looked at me with a sideways glance.

"Yes. Let's get out of here before I get caught."

I leaned over, turned his face toward mine, and kissed him. He revved the engine and headed across the border. We ended up on the road near LeeAnn's uncle's cabin. Arnold parked the car and took a blanket out of his trunk. Then he opened my car door and led me to the blanket. He was a good kisser. I will give him props for that. This was my first time going further than that, so I had little to critique beyond that. It wasn't until after, when we were putting our clothes back on, he spoke.

"Laney is a better kisser than you are, but at least you aren't afraid to go all the way."

I was furious! *How did he know I wasn't Laney?* I needed to play it cool.

"What are you talking about? I am Laney."

"Susie, you didn't think I would notice your sunburn when you were naked? Plus, Laney has an athletic build, you... don't."

He laughed. I couldn't believe he had the audacity to laugh at me. I looked down and saw a rock. His back was to me now as he was pulling up his pants. I needed two hands to lift the rock. One blow, that's all it took to knock him down. The blood seeped out of his ears. I dropped the rock. *What did I do?* Then it hit me.

I didn't do anything. Laney did it. She was the one that had the date with Arnold, not me. No one knew about us and this little rendezvous. But everyone knew about Laney and Arnold's date.

We were leaving the next morning. Hopefully, before anyone discovered Arnold. I dragged his body over to the woods and covered him up with some brush. I threw the rock in the opposite direction. Then I got in his car and drove it an hour away.

I was lucky that eventually; I hitched a ride back to Memere's house. No one was the wiser. I slipped back in through the window and cleaned myself up in the bathroom.

CHAPTER FIFTEEN

HOME SWEET HOME

Scott drove us to the cell phone store and, as promised, got me a new phone. This was perfect because now Laney had no way of communicating with him, if there was any possibility of her using her phone. The new phone took over her old phone. This becoming her was easier than I had thought. Next was the bank to get me a new debit card. I wouldn't be able to get a new driver's license until I went to the DMV the next day. Scott said he had all the information we needed at home in our safe. This was becoming simple.

"Can you tell me what happened yet, Laney?"

"Scott, I am tired. Can we just go home and let me unpack and relax? I will fill you in, I promise. It's just been completely emotionally exhausting."

"Okay, dear. I am just concerned that your friendship of over thirty years has dissolved. It had to be pretty serious for it to end that abruptly."

He was a persistent pain in my ass. I had to distract him from his thoughts, so I placed my hand on his thigh and just rubbed back and forth.

"I don't want to think about all that. I just want to be home with you. That is all I want to think about."

Scott smiled. I knew that would change his train of thought. All men were the same, flirt a little and get them thinking about sex, and viola they totally forgot what they were thinking about before.

Their house was beautiful from the outside. I had seen it the many times I cased it, watching my sister come and go. She frequently sat on the front porch reading while sitting on the porch swing. It amazed me she still pursued the annoy-ing habit of immersing herself in the pages of someone else's imagination. I never understood her obsession with books. Scott pulled into the driveway and then hit the button to open the garage door. He pulled in alongside the SUV my sister usually drove, which would now be mine. It wasn't my Mercedes, but eventually, I would convince him to trade in the SUV for something more my style.

The gentleman, Scott, carried my suitcase into the house. I followed him as he went through the mudroom off the garage and through the kitchen. The layout of the house was an open-floor concept, thankfully. That meant less for me to memorize which room was where. He led me to our master ensuite upstairs above the garage.

It was just as beautiful inside Laney's house as it was outside. Simple, yet well-kept and tidy. Very different from how she had kept her room growing up. As I was assessing the bedroom, Scott came up behind me and encircled my waist with his arms. Then he started planting kisses on the nape of my neck, brushing my hair aside. Just as I was about to turn in his arms and press my lips against his, his arms stiffened and he stopped kissing me.

I turned to look at him and saw some confusion on his face.

"What's the matter, dear? Why did you stop?"

"Nothing, I just remembered that you were exhausted. Why don't you relax and take a bath, then we can resume this afterward."

"Sounds good to me. I will take that bath so we can continue this later."

I reached up and wrapped my arms around his neck and drew him to me. My lips planted on his and I kissed him. That seemed to snap him out of whatever fog he had been in, and he returned the kiss. I had watched my sister do this to him frequently from afar. We broke our embrace and as I turned to walk toward the bathroom; I let my hand trail down his body.

When I got into the bathroom, the lavishness of it blew me away. I never thought my sister would indulge in such luxuries. Scott was still standing in the bedroom, watching me as I entered the bathroom. As I closed the door, I blew him a kiss. The tub was a garden tub with jets, and the shower had two entrances on either side of where the tub was situated. Multiple shower heads were in the shower stall area, leading me to believe two people could shower at once. This was tempting me to ask Scott to join me, but I needed to think up a story to tell him about why I came home.

I filled the tub and enjoyed a nice relaxing soak. My hands and feet were pruned by the time I climbed out. To my surprise and yet relief, Scott was not waiting for me in the bedroom. Wrapped in a towel, I opened my suitcase. To my dismay, Scott had unpacked everything. This left me in a predicament. I did not know which closet was Laney's or which dresser. I quickly opened the closets and figured out which one was my sister's. Then I opened some drawers and found underwear and a nightshirt.

Scott was downstairs on the couch watching television. I sat and snuggled up to him. He responded by putting his arm around me. I figured now would be a good time to tell him the story I had conjured up.

"Now that I have had time to calm down and think through everything that happened. I feel I can share with you, but you have to promise me you won't get mad or do anything."

"Of course, babe. I just want to know the truth."

"Well, I thought we were going to be staying at Memere's house. Instead, LeeAnn brought us to her uncle's hunting cabin. It was filthy. But that's not why I left."

"Okay, so why did you leave?"

"Well, we went out for dinner when we got there at a local bar. I didn't know that LeeAnn had given some guys the address to the cabin when we left."

"Aren't LeeAnn and Cora Lynn both married?"

"Yes! So when these guys showed up, I pulled them both aside and asked them what they were doing. They said, 'having a little fun.' I wasn't having anything to do with it. I would not cheat on you."

"What did they say?"

"They said, ' I was always a prude!' Then they said I better not tell anyone, especially their husbands."

"Then what?"

"That's when I said I was leaving! I grabbed my suitcase and headed out the door. I had walked a couple of miles before I realized I forgot my purse with all my IDs and credit cards back at the cabin. Oh, and my cell phone."

"So you left because they were cheating on their husbands and they called you a prude because you wouldn't join in?"

"Yeah, they know how I feel about cheating. Like, hello, don't they remember my sister and Troy? Sorry, I don't mean to bring up my past boyfriend."

"It's okay, honey. I know you would never cheat on me. I am proud of you for standing up for your beliefs. Are you going to tell Rich and Mike?"

"I don't know. Should I? I mean, I really just want to just keep my distance and stay out of it."

"Well, if someone knew my wife was cheating on me, I would want to know."

"I will think about it."

His arm squeezed me closer to him and he kissed my forehead. His cell phone interrupted us. He looked at it, looked at me, and frowned.

"It's LeeAnn."

"Don't answer it. I want nothing to do with her anymore."

"Okay, babe, whatever you say."

LeeAnn attempted to call him several times, then Cora Lynn did too. They were relentless. Thankfully, Scott listened to me and didn't answer any of their calls. I hadn't thought that they would call him. Then the phone rang again. He didn't recognize the number, so he answered it. His face registered confusion and then anger. From what I could gather from his end of the conversation, it was Laney, but he didn't believe her because I was sitting next to him. When he hung up, he just looked at me.

"Unbelievable! That was LeeAnn or Cora Lynn pretending to be you, saying the cops arrested you for a murder that happened thirty years ago."

I laughed.

"That is insane!"

So, they arrested Laney for Arnold's murder. That was good. The icing on the cake, though, was they had also connected her to Daniel and Troy's murders. That could be a problem for me. That meant national news coverage. I would have to come up with a plan to keep Scott away from the news.

Preemptively, I grabbed his hand as I was getting off the couch. I pulled at him to follow me. Taking my cue, he shut off the tv and followed me to the bedroom. I wrapped my arms around his neck and kissed him, pulling him down with me onto the bed. I lifted his shirt up and over his head, breaking our embrace. His hands ran down my body till he reached the end of my nightshirt. He helped me wiggle out of it, and then looked me up and down. I was just about to wiggle out of my underwear when he abruptly removed himself from the bed and went into the bathroom.

"Is everything okay?"

"Yeah, sorry Laney, my stomach isn't feeling too well. I don't think we can continue this tonight. I am sorry, honey."

"Do you need me to get you anything?"

"No, I will be okay. I just might be in here for a bit. Don't worry, I will turn the fan on."

"Okay, love you."

"Love you too."

I put my nightshirt back on and fell asleep before Scott emerged from the bathroom.

Chapter Sixteen

1988

Road Trip Last Day

The others were up and already packing before I finally awoke. It had been a late night for me. When I finally came out to the kitchen, Laney was the first to say anything.

"Susan, we need to get on the road soon. It is a long drive home and we want to be home before dark."

"Okay, I will go get dressed and pack my suitcases."

She didn't know that I was in just as much of a hurry as she was. I wanted to get out of dodge before the cops found Arnold's abandoned car and before they started looking for Arnold. I packed my suitcases and dressed sooner than I think anyone expected. We said our goodbyes to memere and thanked her for her hospitality.

We were on the road home by ten o'clock in the morning. My palms were getting sweatier the longer we were at memere's house. I relaxed slightly when we were on our way home. After about an hour, I was feeling less tense. The others were singing along to the radio, which was getting pretty annoying. Then Cora Lynn slowed down and LeeAnn turned down the radio. Up ahead, there were several cop cars. As we passed them, it was Laney that broke the silence.

"That looked like Arnold's car! I hope he wasn't in an accident."

"I didn't see any other cars, and I didn't see him either. Maybe he got pulled over for speeding and was in the back of the cruiser?"

"Yeah, you are probably right, LeeAnn."

I knew differently, and my hands were sweating again. I turned to look back at the cops and Arnold's car. The memory of the rock hitting his skull flashed through my mind. Quickly, I turned back to face the road ahead. *It wasn't me. Laney did it.* I said it over and over in my head. The need for me to believe this and convince myself of this would be the basis of my survival. I killed someone, and I needed to make sure I never got caught.

My sister, on the other hand, could go down for it. I would be happy if she got put in jail. Perfect Laney. Straight A, honor society, all-star athlete, Laney. Our parents thought she was a saint, especially since she donated her bone marrow to me when I was ten. They said she saved my life, and I owed her. Yes, I was grateful that she helped to save me from cancer, but to be reminded of it daily was annoying. She complained when I didn't do chores, but that was the only way I could feel special by telling our parents I didn't feel well. That was the only time they treated me as special. No, technically, I wasn't sick anymore. I had been in remission for four years now, but when I said I didn't feel well, I felt seen and heard again.

The lull of the tires on the pavement put me to sleep. When I opened my eyes, it was dark out and the headlights of the oncoming traffic made me blink several times. I looked around the car. Laney was asleep with her head leaning against the window, as was LeeAnn in the front passenger seat. Cora Lynn was the only one awake because she was driving. Our eyes met in the rearview mirror.

"Ah, I see sleeping beauty has woken. Were you dreaming of prince charming? Or Prince Arnold?"

Was she taunting me? Did she know something? My hands were sweating again, and I wiped them on my shorts.

"Oh, definitely prince charming. Arnold is gross."

"Really? Then why were you flirting with him all week?"

"You really have to ask that question? If you must know, I flirted with him to bug Laney. That's all. I had no interest in him."

"Well, you could have fooled me. You were pretty convincing."

"See, I tell everyone I would be a talented actress. This just proves that point."

Laney grumbled and moved in her seat. *Great, the beast is awakening.*

"You aren't a talented actress. You are good at lying, though."

"And please tell Laney, what am I lying about?"

"The better question is, what don't you lie about? It would be easier to answer. It's a shorter list. You liked Arnold and you know it. You flashed him your breasts unless you are willing to admit you are just a slut."

"I am not a slut! I didn't flash him on purpose!"

I crossed my arms over my chest. My thoughts raced to the night before and what I had done with Arnold. How he had kissed me and other things. My cheeks felt flush and butterflies made my belly feel strange. All those things I enjoyed until he compared me to Laney. And then the memory of the rock and what I had done came into my mind. *What Laney had done, not me.*

"Yeah, right. If he had asked you on a date instead of me, you would have jumped at the chance. And if he had tried getting down your pants, you would have let him."

"I would not! Like I said, I just pretended to like him to piss you off and make you jealous. Which clearly I did. I bet you that you let him get in your pants and I bet you loved every minute, but you don't want anyone to know, so you are the one lying."

"You are funny. Why would I punch a guy in the nose and make him bleed after sleeping with him and lie about it all to my best friends?"

"I don't know, Laney. Why do you do some of the stuff you do? Like stealing his car?"

"I didn't steal his car. I borrowed it."

"Yeah, you are certifiably crazy. And a liar."

I was over arguing with my sister. She was crazy and I would make sure people eventually knew it.

CHAPTER SEVENTEEN

EARLY MORNING

I awoke before Scott did and went down to the kitchen to make a cup of coffee. It was a warm fall day, so I had my cup of joe out on the front porch. As I sat on the porch swing, I saw the cable connection box and remembered the dilemma of Laney's arrest, possibly making national news. I unscrewed the connection but made it look like it was still in place. That took care of the tv. But I still had to make sure no one called him or texted him. I knew just the place we could go.

Scott joined me on the porch with a cup of coffee. He peered over his coffee cup at me.

"Did you sleep well, Laney?"

"Yes, I did. How are you feeling? Do you want me to make you some toast? Or can you tolerate eggs as well this morning?"

"I am good. My stomach is still a little queasy though, so I will not kiss you or anything. If I am getting sick, I don't want you to catch it."

"Do you feel well enough to go away for a few days? I don't have to be back at work till next week. My co-worker has a cabin up in New Hampshire. It would be perfect for a little get-away. You know, I could really use some time away just with you."

"Sure, honey. Whatever you want. We should go to the DMV and get your license first."

"Sounds like a plan. I will get the directions from my co-worker and pack. You should pack as well, and then we can head out."

"I am going to finish my coffee first. And try to catch the weather."

I went into the kitchen and washed my coffee cup. Scott went into the living room to turn on the weather. His frustration was evident as he slammed the remote onto the coffee table.

"What's wrong?"

"It seems as if the cable is out."

"Oh, do we need to call the cable company?"

"Nah, I will look and see if the connections are good first."

"Well, do we really need to do it now, since we are going out of town? Can't it wait?"

"I guess it can."

Crisis averted. I didn't need him finding the loose connection outside. I needed to get him out of the house and to the cabin where I could keep him occupied. The cabin wasn't my co-workers. It was mine. There was no tv, no internet, and best of all, no cell service. If I could keep him up there for a few days until I could figure out what I was going to do. I hadn't con-sidered that Laney would get collared for the other two murders and possibly make national headlines. But it was poetic justice that she was being connected to them. It made sense since one had given her his number and the other was her ex-boyfriend. Out of the three, the only one I had a connection with was Troy, but all this time, they never suspected me.

We put the suitcases in Scott's truck and drove to the DMV. He waited outside while I got my new license. Then we headed to the cabin. It took several hours, and we stopped at the grocery store before we drove down the dirt road.

"This cabin is way out here."

"Isn't it great! Just the two of us, no distractions. It can be like a second honeymoon. Unless, of course, you're still not feeling well."

"I am actually feeling better. It sounds like a fun time. Just the two of us."

He reached over and squeezed my thigh and then ran his hand up and down it. It was going to be fun distracting him. Maybe I could get him to stay up here for an extended period. No one expected me back soon. Laney was out of the picture. Our parents thought I was on a business trip. And Scott had told no one we were going anywhere. We could theoretically stay here for weeks. I could have some fun with him.

We unpacked the groceries and settled into the cabin. Scott started a fire in the fireplace and I prepared some pasta for dinner. He seemed so gullible. Clearly, he was madly in love with my sister and treated her like a queen. Typical of Laney to get everything she ever wanted out of life. It was too easy to slide into her life. To some degree, I couldn't believe he hadn't noticed that I was not Laney.

"Dear, I am going to get more firewood for the evening. I will be right back."

Scott approached me and kissed me on the forehead. I had never had a man treat me this way. Most of the men I had dated over the years were the type to screw me, then screw me over. Just like Arnold that very first time. I gave him my virginity and then he mocked me.

"Sure, my love, dinner will be ready soon, so don't be too long."

He smiled at me as he walked out the door. When he came back, he had an armful of split wood that he placed in the wood rack next to the fireplace. I placed two plates full of the meal I had made on the coffee table in front of the fire. When I brought over two glasses of wine, Scott gave me a sweet grin. We sat side by side on the sofa, eating and watching the flames flicker and dance. The flames were mesmerizing, and I daydreamed we could spend the rest of our days together here.

Scott cleared the plates and did the dishes. Then he took the wine glasses and refilled them. The more he did for me, the more I really wanted to keep this charade going. I definitely wanted to find out what his love-making skills were. That would seal the deal. If he was good, then I would keep him. If he was bad, he would wind up like the rest.

"Hey, there is a hot tub out on the deck. Let's go use it."

Scott looked at me with raised eyebrows.

"I didn't bring a bathing suit."

"Neither did I."

I rose from the sofa, holding the glass of wine in one hand, and stretched my other out to him to take. He took it and I led him out onto the deck.

I placed my glass onto the edge of the hot tub and took his and did the same. I stripped down, letting each piece of clothing drop seductively. Scott stood there watching, looking me up and down. He ran his fingers through his hair and slowly undressed. He seemed distracted and nervous.

"What is the matter?"

"Nothing, my dear. Aren't you afraid someone will see us?"

"Here? There is no one around for miles."

I stepped forward and helped him undress. Then we entered the hot tub. The warm water was relaxing and as I sipped my wine, I slid my foot along his leg. He closed his eyes and sat back with a smile on his face. One thing I could say, he wasn't aggressive. He was letting me make all the moves. Most men would have been all over me by now. It was unsettling and refreshing all in one.

As I took another sip of my wine, I felt dizzy. I stopped sliding my foot and grasped the edge of the tub. Scott opened his eyes and sat up.

"What's wrong?"

"I am not feeling so well. I am dizzy and slightly nauseous."

"Well, why don't I carry you to bed?"

"That sounds wonderful."

We climbed out of the hot tub, and he picked me up and carried me to the bed. And that was the last thing I remember until waking up handcuffed to the bedposts. I must have passed out for a bit. Scott was into kink, I supposed. So far, I liked what I was seeing. Although, as I looked around, I didn't see Scott. When he came into the room fully dressed, I was confused. Then I realized I was no longer naked as well.

Scott approached me with a Cheshire cat smile. Then he climbed onto the bed and straddled me. The knife in his hand sent panic throughout my body and I tried to wriggle underneath him.

"I am glad you are awake, dear."

CHAPTER EIGHTEEN

AUGUST 1988

We had been home for a few weeks when it was time for Laney to go to her cross-country camp. It was her second year of attending. This would leave me at home, which infuriated me. There was no way for me to weasel my way to go with her. I didn't do sports. Cora Lynn and LeeAnn drove her there for our parents. It was the second day she was gone that I came across the crumpled piece of paper I had retrieved from the trash on our trip to Canada. I smiled. It was the perfect time to call Daniel. I dialed the number and held my breath as it rang. When he answered, I twirled the phone cord around my finger.

"Hi Daniel, this is Laney. You gave me your number a few weeks ago at the restaurant. "

There was a pause.

"Oh yeah, hi Laney. How are you? When I hadn't heard from you right away, I assumed you weren't interested."

"I am sorry. My sister, Susie, took the piece of paper and hid it from me. I just found it."

"Oh, I get it. I have younger siblings too. I know what a pain they can be."

We talked for an hour or so. Then he had to go to work. The next day he called me and we spoke for a long time as well. He wanted to see me again, in person. I explained that I didn't drive yet, so we made plans to meet at the Norwich-town Mall in a couple of days. It wouldn't be the first time I would walk there. Laney and I had done it on several occasions. She would play at the arcade and I would go to Caldor or Two Legs and try on all the latest fashions.

The day I was meeting Daniel I was careful to dress as my sister would have. I sat on a bench outside of the little greenhouse newsstand that was in the mall and waited. Daniel was punctual.

"Hey Laney, it's great to see you again. Is there a place we can get something to eat around here?"

"Yes, there is BeeBee Dairy. They have the best milkshakes."

It was turning out to be a superb first date. Daniel didn't seem to suspect I wasn't Laney. When we finished our lunch, we walked to the arcade and he held my hand. We played a few games and laughed when we lost. I was truly enjoying myself.

"Laney, is there anywhere we can go where we can be alone?"

My heart raced in my chest. He wanted to be alone with me. Part of me was scared, I didn't know him that long. However, the budding woman in me was excited to be alone with him.

"Sure. I know a few dirt roads. If you are looking for seclusion."

"Perfect, let's get out of here."

His car was a beat-up pickup truck. Not at all what I expected. I gave him the directions to the dirt road, and he parked his truck. When he put his arm around me and pulled me closer, I knew I was in for some fun. He was an excellent kisser, much better than Arnold. At least this time, there was no chance of Daniel comparing me to my sister. I had heard stories from my friends about having sex in the backseat of a car. I had heard none of it being done in the front seat of a truck.

It wasn't comfortable, that was for sure. But it was exciting. When we finished, he drove me home. We talked on the phone twice after and then he came to visit again. This time, he picked me up at my house. I thought we would go hang out for a bit first, then go have some privacy. Daniel had other plans. He drove straight to the dirt road. At least this time he brought a blanket, and we got out of the truck. It was a little walk to where he placed the blanket.

This time was even more enjoyable considering the comfort level was better. We did things we hadn't done the first time, and I really liked it. As soon as we were done though Daniel stood up and started putting his pants on.

"Are you in a hurry to leave?"

"Laney, I need to get home, I have to work."

"You didn't tell me that. I thought we were going to spend the day together like we did last time. You know, like a date. I don't mind having sex beforehand, but I feel a bit used right now, instead of being your girlfriend."

"Whoa. Who said anything about you being my girlfriend? We are just having some fun. Nothing serious. I go back to college in a week or two. Out in California."

I was seeing red. He used me for sex, nothing more. I noticed he hadn't picked up his belt yet. He was bending over to grab his shirt. In one swift motion, I grabbed the belt and wrapped it around his neck from behind him, and pulled as tight as I could, until his body went limp and crashed to the ground. I dragged his body further from the road and then drove his truck a few miles away. Then I walked home. It was when I was home and in the bath that I realized I had somehow gotten a scratch on my leg.

A week later, there had been a newspaper article about the body of an unidentified male being found. It wasn't for a couple of days later that they found the truck and they had made an identification. They ruled the death a homicide, but there were no leads in the case.

CHAPTER NINETEEN

SCOTT'S REVELATON

At first, I didn't know what to think when my usually calm, under any circumstances, wife called me in hysterics from the bus station. Something terrible must have happened between her and her two best friends for her to be this upset. So I rushed to the bus station to get her. I knew right away the woman that I picked up wasn't my wife. There were subtle differences in her appearance, but I knew Laney. We had been together for over twenty years. We had three beautiful daughters together. Thankfully, they were away at college because I did not know the intentions of this woman. Laney and I had built a life together. This woman wasn't her.

Laney had a knack about her, especially when facing even the most ferocious storms of staying extremely level-headed. One of her most endearing qualities was that she communicated with me about everything. Even on those days when she wasn't happy with me. The fact that this woman wouldn't tell me what had occurred between her and her friends was a huge red flag.

Whatever game this woman was playing with me, I knew I needed to play along. If she was impersonating my wife, I needed to know what really happened to the real Laney. When I kissed this imposter on the neck and brushed her hair aside, that was the first confirmation that she was absolutely not my Laney. Laney had an Aquarius symbol tattooed on the nape of her neck. This woman did not. My body and mind betrayed my intent to act as if I had no clue that this woman was not who she claimed to be. She had picked up on my change of attitude. It was quick thinking on my part to suggest she take a relaxing bath.

Thankfully, she responded positively to the suggestion. While she was in the bath, I unpacked her things. They were definitely not Laney's possessions. I had never seen any of these articles of clothing before. Since I help my wife with laundry regularly, I am pretty aware of her wardrobe. These were the types of clothes she would wear, but my wife had never actually worn them. This was a relief to me. At least partially. It meant that this imposter hadn't had contact with my wife, or so it would seem. Even the suitcase was not actually Laney's. We had a habit of writing brief notes to each other on stickers and affixing them to the inside of each other's suitcases when one of us had to go out of town without the other. This suitcase had none.

I did not know what I was going to do. The thought of calling the police crossed my mind, but I still didn't know if Laney was safe and alive. Just thinking about the possibility of living my life without her resolved me to find out who this imposter was first. I had my suspicions. Even though I had never met Laney's sister Susan in our entire relationship, I knew she resembled my wife enough to potentially try something like this.

My in-laws rarely shared information about Susan with Laney and me. We knew Susan had been married twice, and that was it. Their parents had come to terms with their daughter's strained relationship years ago. When we went to visit, they removed all pictures of Susan out of respect for Laney's wishes. Neither of us knew if Susan still resembled Laney. I had to know what she looked like presently, so I texted my mother-in-law while the imposter was in the bath.

Hey Mom. I got a favor to ask. It may sound odd.

Okay? What is the favor?

Do you have a recent picture of Susan? I was out doing errands today and could have sworn I saw Laney, but as you know, she is in Canada. So I was thinking maybe I saw Susan and didn't even realize it.

Susan is out of the country on a business trip.

Well, this was turning out to be harder than I thought, but if the woman in my house was Susan, it would make sense that she would tell her parents she was going on a trip.

Oh, well, can you send me a pic of her, anyway? It's driving me crazy thinking there is someone that looks almost identical to Laney around town.

Sure. Give me a minute and I will send you the most recent one I have.

It took a few minutes, but my mother-in-law came up with the picture. It was amazing how alike my wife and her sister looked. Especially for not being actual twins. This was certainly the woman in my house, but I couldn't tell her mother that.

Thanks. It isn't the same person I saw, but wow, it is crazy how much Susan looks like Laney.

I was on the couch when Susan came down and snuggled up against me. This made my skin crawl. *How was I supposed to play off that I sus-pected nothing when I knew this woman was not my wife?* Susan told me her far-fetched story about LeeAnn and Cora Lynn wanting to cheat on their husbands. It was hard to not call her out for her lies. Cora Lynn's husband had died in a car crash six months ago and LeeAnn was in the middle of a divorce. So, even if they had invited some men to the cabin, I knew this wouldn't have upset Laney.

As I tried to play the comforting husband, that's when LeeAnn and Cora Lynn started to blow up my phone. Susan insisted that I not answer their calls. It was when the unidentified number came up that my stomach did flips. When I an-swered the phone and heard my wife's voice, relief washed over me she was alive. It confused me they had arrested her for someone's murder and possibly two other murders. The imposter was sitting right next to me and I didn't know her end game.

Laney was safe, and that was all that mattered, so I needed to figure out what Susan was up to. When she led me back to the bedroom, I physically felt ill kissing her. Then, while she was there, naked in front of me, it solidified that this woman was not my wife. I knew every inch of Laney. Her tattoos, the stretch marks from carrying our beautiful daughters, and the scars from the double mastectomy and reconstructive surgery she had had.

Getting ill was a godsend. It gave me a way out from actually having to do anything with this woman. I brought my phone with me to the bathroom and texted LeeAnn and Cora Lynn about the predicament I was in. I told them both to tell Laney I loved her and that I would do everything I could to get her set free. Then I texted my daughters to tell them about their mother and to apprise them of the situation here at home. I begged them to not text or call their mother's cell phone and not to come home until I let them know it was safe to do so.

CHAPTER TWENTY

SUMMER OF 1992

Since my graduation party, Laney and I had not spoken to each other. Troy and I continued to see each other. We were a couple for a year and I was daydreaming of the day he would propose to me as I got ready for our year anniversary date. He had made reservations at the Yantic River Inn. When he picked me up, it disappointed me he hadn't brought me flowers.

"What, no flowers? You know how much I love roses."

"I am sorry Susan. I forgot how much they mean to you."

We walked to his car, and he got in without opening my car door for me. I scowled at him as I got in.

"What? What did I do now?"

"It isn't what you did, it's what you didn't do. You can't even be bothered with opening my car door for me."

"I am sorry Susan. I just have a lot on my mind."

A lot on his mind? I wonder if he is going to propose to me.

I lean over to him and give him a kiss on the cheek while rubbing his thigh.

"Oh, I am sorry. It's just that tonight is special and I want to make sure it's perfect."

Troy gave me a nervous smile before we drove off to the restaurant. He was mindful to open my car door, held the restaurant door, and even pulled my chair out for me. I waited impatiently throughout our entire meal for him to ask me that all-important question. So when he asked for the check from the waiter without doing so, I was a bit confused. We went to our usual make-out spot and he still didn't propose. It wasn't until we got back to the driveway of my house that I thought maybe, this was it.

"Susan, we really need to talk. I know I have been a bit distracted tonight, and I am sorry."

This was it, he was going to propose.

"It's okay Troy, baby."

"Susan, I was offered a new job, but it means I have to move to Virginia. It's making more money. It is better for my future."

"You mean our future, right?"

Where was he going with this conversation?

"No, Susan. My future. We don't have a future. It's been fun and all, but you are not the type of girl I want for a wife."

I couldn't believe what I was hearing. I wasted an entire year with this guy. The rage was building inside me, but we were sitting in my driveway. There was nothing I could do. I got out of the car and slammed the door. He would pay, not tonight, but eventually, he would pay.

He was living in his own apartment already, so it was pretty easy to stalk him. I found out through casual conversations with mutual friends when he was moving and where he was moving to. I didn't let anyone know how upset I was about our breakup. When it came up in conversation, I made it sound like I was happy for him. I even started dating someone else. His name was Paul. This was just so no one would suspect me. I begged my new boyfriend to take me on a trip to Virginia Beach the weekend Troy was moving.

I showed up at Troy's apartment and knocked on the door.

"Susan, what are you doing here?"

"I know you and I broke up and everything, but I didn't know where else to go."

I cried and spun a tale of how my current boyfriend had abused me. This was an issue I knew would spin Troy up because he had seen his mother abused at the hands of his stepfa-ther.

"Where is this bastard?"

"I left him at the hotel."

"Let's go."

I directed Troy to where I wanted him to go. It wasn't the hotel. It was an old back road. When I told him to stop and he put his car in park, he looked at me with an expression of confusion.

That's when I pulled out the knife and stabbed him in the heart repeatedly. It was such a mess. I was thankful for two things. One, there was a creek nearby where I could wash the blood off myself and my clothes, and two, it was a hot summer night. I walked most of the way back to the hotel and, as I did, my clothes dried.

When I got to the hotel, I threw the knife in the dumpster. Back in the hotel room where my boyfriend was drunk and passed out, I took a shower and changed my clothes. It was then I noticed the cut on my hand. I must have cut myself as I was stabbing Troy. I rolled my dirty clothes up and put them in my suitcase. Then I climbed into bed with my unsuspecting alibi.

It was weeks later that I got a visit from the police. They were questioning all of Troy's old friends and acquaintances about his death. I played the devastated ex-girlfriend well. I think because they never bothered me again.

Paul and I continued to date for the rest of the summer.

CHAPTER TWENTY-ONE

SCOTT'S PLAN

In the morning, Susan had let me sleep, thankfully. I didn't want to have to touch her or show affection toward her. When I came downstairs and found her on the porch drinking coffee, I laughed to myself. Susan truly didn't know her sister. Laney didn't drink coffee. She actually hated everything about it: the smell, the taste, and even the mess the coffee grounds made.

It didn't surprise me in the least when I went to turn on the TV that the cable wasn't working. No doubt that Susan didn't want me to see the news about Laney and her arrest. When she asked to go away to New Hampshire, it fit into my plans to confront her. She didn't seem to suspect a thing that I was on to her. While she was in the shower, I kept LeeAnn and Cora Lynn in the loop through texts.

When we got to the cabin and I realized there was no cell service, I had a minor panic attack. My plan was to get her drunk to the point I could tie her up and confront her. She had played right into my hands with the hot tub and wine. I managed to handcuff her to the bed when she passed out. When she awoke, I straddled her with a knife in my hand, ready to confront her. Susan's eyes were wide open with the realization she had nowhere to go.

"Scott, honey, what are you doing? You are scaring me."

"Don't honey me, Susan. And I hope I am scaring you because I want to know why the hell are you pretending to be Laney?"

"Honey, what are you talking about? I am Laney. I am your wife. You said so when Cora Lynn and LeeAnn tried pretending to be me."

"Susan, I know you are not Laney. I have known all along. You are nothing like her."

"You are right Scott, I am nothing like my sister. Let me loose and I will show you all how I am so much better."

The switch in her demeanor was scary. She was clearly a psychopath.

"That will not happen. I love my wife and every time I kissed you, I had to refrain from vomiting. I needed you to believe I didn't suspect you."

This made Susan mad, and she writhed underneath me.

"How did you know I wasn't Laney?"

"First of all, Laney would never call me up hysterical crying, ever. Then it was your lack of certain tattoos that Laney has and scars."

"My sister has tattoos? That is surprising and something I never considered. What scars does she have?"

"Yes, she has tattoos. We actually have matching ones of our birth sign. And yes she has scars from her battle with breast cancer two years ago."

"My sister had breast cancer? How come nobody told me?"

"Only those closest to her knew."

"Our parents? Did they know?"

"Of course they did. Laney asked them not to tell you."

"And, of course, they would listen to Laney."

"So Susan, why this charade?"

I waved the knife in the air as I asked, and her eyes followed it carefully.

"Why? Because it is fun pretending to be my sister. I have done it for years. That is how I got Troy in the first place. The first few times we were together he thought I was Laney. And then he enjoyed having me around more than her because I would do things she wouldn't."

"But why now? You are both grown adults, why would you try to take over her life now."

"Why not? She will be going to jail for murders she didn't commit and you will need someone to take care of your needs. I am the right person for the job."

"How do you know she will go to jail for those murders?"

"She is the only person tied to all three and since they have DNA evidence linking her to them, I am pretty sure it's a sure thing she will get convicted."

Susan laughed. She was crazy. And then I realized.

"You killed those guys, didn't you?"

"Nope, Laney did it."

"You just said, ' It's fun being, Laney.' You pretended to be her, didn't you? And you killed them."

"Nope. I already told you, Laney did it. Laney is a murderer, not me."

"Okay, so how did Laney murder those guys? And why?"

Susan laughed maniacally and then recounted every detail of the three murders they charged Laney with. I wish I had recorded it on my phone, but I hadn't even thought of it until after she lay beneath me, continuing to laugh.

I had to get the sheriff. They needed to arrest Susan, and then Laney would be set free. My cell phone had no service. There was no landline.

The only way to summon the police would be to drive into town. That meant leaving Susan handcuffed to the bed. I made sure the handcuffs were as tight as possible and I tied her feet to the footboard.

"I am going to get the police. You will be arrested. I am going to tell them that you confessed to the murders in great detail. And Laney will be set free."

Susan stopped laughing. Rage filled her and she writhed on the bed trying to somehow set herself free.

"There is no use. You are just going to hurt yourself. The game is up Susan."

I grabbed my keys and headed to my truck. Susan's frantic screams echoed behind me. The town was a half hour away. It was dark and I took it slow down the winding dirt driveway to the main road.

CHAPTER TWENTY-TWO

SUMMER OF 1993

Paul and I eloped a year after our trip to Virginia. He inherited a cabin in New Hampshire when his grandpa died. My parents hated Paul. They were always comparing him to Laney's boyfriend, Scott. Just as I couldn't live up to their expectations and comparisons to Laney. Paul would never compare to Scott in their eyes.

We didn't care; we were in love with each other and we lived our lives the way we wanted to. That meant we smoked a lot of weed and drank a lot of alcohol. Most of our friend group partied too. There was one party where I caught Paul having a little too much fun with one of my friends.

"What are you doing?"

They were both intoxicated.

"Oh, Susan. I am so sorry. We didn't mean for anything to happen. It's just we are drunk, and we wanted to go in the hot tub."

My friend piped up.

"And we didn't have any bathing suits. So we went in naked. Just one thing led to another. We are so sorry."

"I forgive you both."

At least that's what I told them the first time. After the second time, they had to be punished.

It was shortly after that second time; I moved back to my hometown. When anyone asked about Paul, I just said we separated and I hadn't heard from him in a long time. Nobody asked about my friend Missy.

Then I met Kevin. He was smart and funny. Everything I had ever wanted in a man. He helped me get my real estate license, and we became partners. His wife was pleasant, but so naïve. She did not know that I wanted her husband and I always got what I wanted. I had flowers sent to his wife by a secret admirer. Every time he confronted her, and she denied knowing who it was, he would come to me to vent.

"It happened again! Wendy received flowers from someone. She claims she has no clue who they are from."

"Do you think she is capable of cheating on you?"

"I don't know. I never thought so before now."

He put his hands over his face and tried to fight back the tears.

"I love her so much. I don't understand why she would do this?"

I put my arm around his shoulder and leaned my head on him.

"I am sorry. You are a great guy and I don't know why she doesn't see that."

His hands dropped from his face, and he looked at me.

"Really?"

"Yes, really. If you weren't married, I would be all about trying to get with you. But you are married and I respect that."

I lifted my head up and ever so gently took my arm off his shoulder, brushing my hand along his arm. As my hand brushed his hand, he grabbed it.

"What's good for the goose is good for the gander, right?"

I took my hand from his.

"I couldn't do that. Never would I want to be a home wrecker!"

"You can't wreck a home that is already wrecked."

That was the beginning of a beautiful relationship. The longest one I ever had. I helped him through his divorce. We moved up to the cabin in New Hampshire that Paul had left me so graciously. My parents actually approved of Kevin. He was business minded. There were fewer comparisons between Kevin and Scott. They were also proud of me, finally, because I had turned out to be a damn good real estate agent.

Laney still wouldn't forgive me or talk to me, though. It didn't bother me as much then because I was happy in all other aspects of my life.

I had Kevin, and finally my parent's approval and acceptance. I didn't need her.

CHAPTER TWENTY-THREE

THE POLICE STATION

When I arrived at the police station, I feared there was no one there. It seemed deserted as I opened the door and the little bell jingled. A tired-looking deputy sat up from behind his desk where he had been reclining.

"How can I help you, sir?"

"I know this is going to sound crazy, but I need you to come with me. My sister-in-law confessed to me about committing multiple murders. Murders that my wife, Laney Wilson, is currently being held in Canada for doing."

"Sir, where is this supposed serial killer now?"

I ran my fingers through my hair and stuffed my hands back into my pockets.

"I handcuffed her back at the cabin we are staying in."

The deputy stood up and put his hat on his head.

"You mean to tell me you unlawfully restrained a woman? That you claim to have committed the murders your wife is being accused of committing? Are you aware of how that sounds?"

"Yes, sir. I am aware. She was trying to impersonate my wife. I knew it wasn't her. When I received a phone call from my actual wife, I knew she was safe. So I had to figure out what this person's end game was. I know it sounds crazy, but please. The sooner we get back to the cabin and you arrest her, the sooner my wife can go free."

"Okay, but I am calling in backup on this. And I am calling the sheriff."

"I am fine with that, but can we please hurry?"

The deputy ushered me to his patrol car, and I sat in the passenger seat. I showed him the way to the cabin. On the way, he radioed his colleagues the entire drive. The driveway was dark and creepy as we approached the cabin. I hoped this nightmare would be over soon and I can get to Laney. When I was at the police station, I texted LeeAnn and Cora Lynn a brief update.

The police cruiser stopped.

"Mr. Wilson, I want you to stay here. Do you understand? If this woman is as dangerous as you claim she is, this is the safest place for you. My backup is pulling in right now. We are going to go in and assess the situation."

"Okay, sir. I will stay right here."

I watched as the deputy and a few others conversed before splitting up. Some went around to the back door and the others went in the front. I saw lights go on throughout the cabin as they cleared each room and entered the back bedroom where I had left Susan. It was the sheriff that came out first, looking confused. He approached the cruiser and opened the door.

"Mr. Wilson, I need you to come with me. We have some questions for you."

"Sure."

As I got out of the cruiser, the sheriff led me into the cabin and to the back bedroom. What I saw didn't make any sense. There in the bed, where I had left Susan handcuffed to the bedposts, were two empty cuffs hanging and blood smeared on the white sheets. I covered my face with my hands and rubbed briskly, hoping to erase what I was seeing.

"Mr. Wilson, do you mind telling us whose blood that is? And where this supposed killer is?"

"Sir, I do not know whose blood it is. I left my sister-in-law right here, yes, tied up because she had confessed to killing three men. The three men my wife is currently being accused of killing. Those handcuffs were as tight as possible. I don't know how she could have gotten free!"

"Mr. Wilson, until we can determine whose blood this is and the whereabouts of your sister-in-law, we are going to ask you to come down to the station while we investigate this further."

"Am I being arrested?"

"No, not at this time. But your cooperation in this matter will go a long way with us."

"Should I be getting a lawyer?"

"You might want to."

The deputy took me back to the station, where they allowed me to call a lawyer from a small conference room. I also texted LeeAnn and Cora Lynn about my predicament. Hours later, the sheriff came in and sat down across from me.

"Mr. Wilson, we didn't find your sister-in-law. Our forensics team is going over the cabin dusting for fingerprints and hair samples. And of course, they are going to analyze the blood. Our K9 uncovered something interesting in the basement of the cabin, though. There were three shallow graves. Do you know anything about those?"

"Sir, I have no idea about the graves. My sister-in-law had said the cabin was a co-worker's. I have never been there before. Are you putting out an APB on her? She is dangerous."

"Mr. Wilson, I have no proof that this woman is a danger to anyone. All I currently have is your word, a blood-smeared bed, and three skeletal remains in a basement. For all I know, you could have killed those three people and attempted to kill her as well. So I am going to ask you to sit tight until we get some answers from forensics."

"Am I being arrested?"

"Not at this time."

"Is it okay if I just stay here? It's late. I have no idea if I can get a room anywhere and quite frankly, with her on the loose, I feel safer here."

"Sure. It will make our job easier if we need to ask you any more questions or if we need to arrest you."

I knew they viewed me as a suspect. I didn't care. Susan was crazy, and I knew she would want revenge for tying her up.

SUMMER OF 2003

Kevin and I had been married for five blissful years. My parents still loved him, and still rarely compared us to Laney and Scott, except in the last five years we had been increasingly hounded by them about when we were going to have kids. That was one thing I loved the most about Kevin. Neither of us had any interest in being parents. Kids would cramp our lifestyle. When we weren't working hard selling real estate, we were jet-setting around the world. Those things would end if we had kids. I didn't want to be a mom. Children repulsed me. The snotty noses. I couldn't imagine having to listen to whining and crying constantly. So I had been so happy when Kevin and I were on the same page on the subject. He was blissfully unaware that I had gotten pregnant at least once every year for the first five years of our marriage. I had taken care of the problem each time. No need to involve him in the decision.

Then one evening on our way home from my parents, after dinner, he had asked the fateful question that I thought we had settled years earlier.

"Susan, maybe we should re-evaluate our position on having kids?"

"Are you serious? I thought we both agreed children were not in our future."

"I don't know. That was five years ago, babe. Think about how awesome it would be to have a mini-me or mini-you running around."

The thought repulsed me. I didn't want to give up the hourglass figure I had worked so hard to get. Let alone the career that had taken me out of my dear sister's shadow. But I didn't want to lose Kevin either. So I reluctantly agreed to go ahead and try to conceive. Now, five years later and no baby, we sat in the office of our new fertility specialist.

"Well, Mr. and Mrs. Johnson, I have all the results of your tests. Mr. Johnson, your sperm count is adequate, and there seem to be no mobility issues."

Kevin's shoulders lifted and fell as he let out a sigh of relief.

"Then why haven't we been able to conceive, doc?"

"Well, your wife's eggs seem fine. However, the results of the hysteroscopy show significant scarring of the uterine walls. Your wife has Asherman Syndrome."

"What does that mean? What causes this?"

Kevin reached for my hand and held it tight. I think he thought I would be upset at hearing this news. Instead, it was a relief. I couldn't have children. This was perfect. That would shut up my parents and Kevin and I could go back to not wanting children.

"What it means is the chances of carrying a pregnancy to term are slim. If you manage to conceive a child, the risk of miscarriage or still-birth is increased. The cause is generally from surgery such as a D&C, a uterine infection, and or radiation therapy."

The look on Kevin's face was one of confusion and sadness. I had never seen him so disappointed. This was the moment I realized how much he truly wanted a child. My heart sank. I knew this was the beginning of the end. He squeezed my hand harder.

"Doc. excuse my ignorance, but what kind of surgery is a D&C?"

Of course, he would ask this question. My heart raced. I, of course, knew what it was, and I knew I had many over the years, but I didn't want Kevin to find that out. So I took the focus off of his question and asked one of my own.

"Doc, you say radiation therapy could cause this? Does that mean the radiation therapy I received as a child before my bone marrow transplant could have caused this?"

I managed to produce some tears in my eyes for added effect. Kevin let go of my hand and wrapped his arm around my shoulder protec-tively.

"Mrs. Johnson, unfortunately, yes. The treat-ment that saved your life so many years ago could have caused the scarring. Thus, rendering your uterus unfit for sustaining another life in-side it. The reason I did the hysteroscopy was because of your medical history and those treat-ments. As for your question, Mr. Johnson, a D&C is a type of surgery used to scrape the lining of the uterus. They use it after miscarriages, to remove fibroids, and for elective abortions."

Thank god the good doctor emphasized he felt the cause of the scarring was from my prior radi-ation treatments. Kevin pulled me tighter to him and I put my head on his shoulder.

"So what you are saying, doc, is that there is no chance of my wife and I conceiving a child the good old-fashioned way?"

"Well, it isn't impossible, but it is highly unlike-ly. You could try having surgery to remove the scarring, but we recommend you wait a year afterward to conceive. You have other options you could consider. Like surrogacy or adoption."

"I don't want to have surgery and then have to wait a year to find out if we can conceive. That would be heart-wrenching."

I turned my head and looked up at Kevin. I blinked my eyelids, pretending to hold back the tears.

"I agree, Susan. I don't want to put you through that. We can discuss the other options at home. Thank you doc, for all your help."

We both rose from our seats and shook the doctor's hand. There was silence between us as we walked out of the medical building and got in our car. Kevin was processing everything. I could see it. It wasn't until we were at home that he broke the silence.

"Susan, have you given any thought to the options the doctor told us about?"

I really hadn't. In my mind, the subject was closed. I couldn't have children. We should just move on and continue with how things already were. But, I couldn't tell him that. He had become invested in the idea of being a dad.

"Honey, I am not sure if either option is the right thing for us. I have heard horror stories about surrogate mothers wanting to keep the baby after carrying it the nine months. And with adoption, well babies are in high demand, so there is so much competition. And there is no way I want to adopt an older child. There is too much of a chance of that child having issues. I don't have the patience for that."

"I am sure there are legal stipulations we can put in place with a surrogate. If they use my sperm and your egg, the mother has no legal right to the child."

He was annoying me. I didn't want a child in any shape or form. I wanted my freedom. This was not an issue that I could see going away. I knew I would miss Kevin. We had a great run.

"I don't know. Let me think about it. I am going to make us some dinner. We can discuss it more when we eat."

Dinner was quiet. I had served wine with it. Kevin was in a subdued mood. When we went to bed, he was drowsier than normal and he was quick to fall asleep. As I watched the rise and fall of his chest slow, then stop, I cried. He was the only one I regretted having to say goodbye to. The basement of the cabin was cold and damp. I picked up the shovel and dug the hole. When I dragged his body down there and covered it up with the dirt, I realized I needed some time away. A vacation was in order, so when the task was complete, I went upstairs and I booked a trip to Europe.

When I returned from the trip, I told everyone Kevin had left me because we couldn't have children of our own. My parents were so sympathetic. I told them I didn't need anyone else in my life now. That I was going to focus on my career and build the business that Kevin had left me.

PART THREE

COMING TOGETHER

"Rather than love, than money, than fame, give me truth."
~ Henry David Thoreau

CHAPTER TWENTY-FIVE

SUSAN'S ESCAPE

Damn it, Scott. Why did you have to ruin a good thing? I didn't think he was smart enough to figure out I wasn't Laney. I guess I was wrong. He had left me handcuffed to the bedposts and went to get the sheriff. The realization hit me I needed to be gone before they got back. I smiled wryly, remembering the few times Paul had used handcuffs during some of our more kinky love making sessions. It had been a while since I last slipped out of handcuffs; I wasn't sure I could do it anymore. The handcuffs were tight, probably the tightest I had ever had a pair on for. It would be a challenge for me to get out of them, but I needed to try. I maneuvered my right hand first, folding my thumb towards my pinky finger. From my vantage point, it looked like I could do this enough to make my hand as wide as my wrist.

As I slowly wriggled my hand through the cuffs, I cut my wrist a little. Soon my first hand was free. I did the same thing with my left hand. My knuckles proved to be a bit of a challenge going through the cuff, and they bled. When that hand was free, I untied my feet, then I wiped my bloody hands all over the sheets. My imagination went wild with the thought of the police coming upon this scene. *Payback is a bitch, Scotty boy, and I can be the biggest bitch around.*

I was fully aware my time was running out, so I quickly grabbed a coat and shoes. My purse was on the counter. I rummaged through it to grab my Laney identification, but couldn't find it. The bastard had taken it with him. *Great, I don't have any identification at all.* I couldn't dwell on it. He had even taken the new cell phone he had gotten me. I packed a backpack with a few items of clothes and a few snacks and headed out of the cabin and into the woods. I knew the direction I needed to head towards to hit a road. It wouldn't be the first time I hitchhiked. Every time I thought about what the police would find back at the cabin, I broke out in laughter. I imagined the police handcuffing Scott because I was sure they would suspect him of hurting whoever he had handcuffed to that bed.

The leaves crunched under each of my footsteps, but I didn't care. There was no one out there but me. Some sadness crept up on me at the realization I could never go back to my cabin. With Scott bringing the police there, I was sure they would investigate things and find my hidden secrets. This made me think of Kevin and how much I missed him. He had been my one true love.

I finally reached the back road that led away from the cabin and the town. It was dark and desolate. I had walked a couple of miles before I heard the rumble of an engine coming up behind me. I turned to face the oncoming headlights and stuck my thumb out, showing I was looking for a ride. The truck slowed and as the passenger side window slid down, the man with the green ball cap leaned over to talk to me.

"Where is a beauty like you headed?"

"Anywhere. but here. Where are you going?"

"I am heading just over the border to my place in Vermont. Does that sound like a place you would like to go to?"

"Sure does. Like I said, anywhere but here."

"Hop on in."

His truck wasn't brand new, but it was fairly clean. It actually smelled of bleach, which I thought was a bit odd. Beggars couldn't be choosers, though, and it was a ride out of this place. The more distance I put between myself and my cabin, the better chance I had of staying free.

"Thanks for the ride. I was getting blisters on my feet."

"No problem, little lady. I am happy to oblige."

I hadn't realized how tired I was until I was staring out the windshield, watching the yellow line whiz by. Soon I had nodded off to sleep. I don't even know how long I was asleep for, but

I awoke to the sensation of the truck slowing down.

"Hey sleeping beauty, glad to see you finally awake. I am stopping for some fuel and food. You want anything?"

"No, thank you. I have got no money on me."

"My treat."

"Okay, thanks."

As promised, he came back with food for the both of us. We sat in the gas station parking lot and ate. Then we were on our way again. I guess he was tired of the silence between us and struck up a conversation.

"So, what are you running away from?"

"What makes you think I am running away from something?"

"Well, no money, a backpack, and you are hitchhiking. Those are classic signs of running away."

"If you must know, I am running away from an abusive ex. He tied me up and left me for dead."

"Oh wow, that sounds horrible. I am sorry that happened to you. You know hitchhiking is dangerous, though, right?"

"Yeah, I know, but not as dangerous as I am."

I chuckled. *If he only knew how true that statement was.* He just looked at me.

"Aren't you afraid of being picked up by a serial killer or something?"

"No. Those odds are improbable."

"What odds?"

"The odds of two serial killers being in the same vehicle at the same time."

He laughed.

"You are feisty. I like that. So when we get to Vermont, what are your plans?"

"I really don't have any plans as yet. I am just flying by the seat of my pants."

"Well, you are more than welcome to stay with me for as long as it takes for you to figure out what your plans are."

"Thanks, I think I would like that."

It was a few more hours before we reached his cabin in the woods of Vermont. It put my cabin to shame. My cabin had been a small one-floor cabin whereas his was a two-story one with a wrap-around porch. It was cozy looking. I could definitely see myself living here. As we got inside, the urge to stay here became greater.

"Here, follow me upstairs. I will show you to your room."

"Thank you."

I followed him up the stairs to a bedroom in the back of the cabin. He ushered me in and I followed him. He showed me the bathroom off the bedroom. This was nice. Then he left me alone and closed the door behind him. It wasn't until I heard the slight click I realized he had locked me inside. I panicked and ran to the window. I pulled back the curtains and pulled up the blinds. To my horror, I realized it really wasn't a window. He trapped me!

"What are you doing? Let me out!"

I banged on the door. I could hear him laughing.

"Not a chance, pretty one. You are mine now."

FORENSICS DON'T LIE

I spent the night at the county sheriff's office in a small, empty jail cell. The deputy had left it unlocked since I wasn't technically under arrest. It was the sheriff, though, that came to wake me up.

"Mr. Wilson, I need you to come with me."

I groggily followed him back into the small conference room he had questioned me in the night before.

"Do I need my lawyer, sheriff?"

"Honestly, I am not sure. I have never had to deal with a case like this before. I don't even know where to start."

"Sir, I know it's confusing. I am telling the truth, though. My sister-in-law confessed to murdering three men in her past."

"Yeah, I verified your story about your wife being accused and arrested for three murders. They have DNA evidence linking her to all three crime scenes. Forensics don't lie. At least that is what we have always thought. This case is testing that theory."

The sheriff scratched his head as he read through a file in front of him.

"Did you find out whose blood it was back at the cabin? I am guessing it was my sister-in-law's, right?"

"Well, not exactly. That has us all confused. The forensics came back as a match for your wife. But your wife has been in custody in Canada for a few days now and that was fresh blood. So it couldn't possibly be your wife's blood."

"Wait, the blood on the bed at the cabin matched my wife? How? That was not my wife."

"Of course, it wasn't your wife. Your wife is in custody. I have forensics testing everything again because it makes little sense. We are still trying to identify the bodies in the basement. Or should I say bones?"

"What does that mean for me?"

"Well, we found no evidence of you ever being in the cabin's basement. Your fingerprints are everywhere upstairs. Thank you for voluntarily providing us with a sample last night, so we can't connect you to the bodies down there. With the blood being your wife's and we have proof she is alive, we have no evidence you committed any crime. We can't hold you, so you are free to go, but please give us a way of contacting you."

"But what about Susan?"

"What about her? We have no proof that she committed a crime, other than what she sup-posedly told you. The cabin is owned by Paul Smith, but no one has seen or heard from him in decades. Everyone thought he had sold the cabin years ago."

"Paul Smith? He owned that cabin?"

"Yeah, did you know him?"

"No, I never met him. My wife had been estranged from her sister for a long time, but her parents would tell us about Susan every once in a while. Paul Smith was Susan's first husband. According to her, they separated."

"Oh, that might change things. That also might give us a lead on at least one body identity. You said Susan's first husband. She had more than one?"

"Yes, her second husband was Kevin Johnson. He left her when they found out they couldn't have kids."

"Thanks for the information. Do you mind sticking around a little longer? I may have some more questions for you."

"Sure. I just want to set my wife free."

"Well, I have already been in contact with the Canadian officials because the blood down here matching your wife adds doubt to their entire case."

"That's great news!"

"Yes, but it makes no sense at all."

"No, it really doesn't. Hopefully, this nightmare will be over soon."

I had asked if I could leave the station to grab a bite to eat and the sheriff said I could. It was a small town with not much for choices. I found a small corner diner. As I sat there eating, I kept mulling over everything that had happened over the last few days. *How could Laney's blood be on the bed in the cabin? That was not Laney, it was Susan. They aren't identical twins. How could Susan's blood match Laney's?* And then it hit me. *The bone marrow transplant. Laney had donated her bone marrow to Susan when they were children.* I had to get back to the sheriff's office. I flagged down my waitress and paid my bill. Then I rushed back to the station.

As I walked in, the sheriff was standing with more paperwork in his hands and shaking his head. He looked up when I came in.

"Mr. Wilson, good news, I guess. Forensics verified it was your wife's blood on the bed in the cabin. We can't explain it. The Canadian authorities have no case against your wife without that

DNA evidence. She has an alibi for the time-frames of the murders as well. So they have no case against her and have no choice except to set her free."

"Sir, I don't know if it is possible because I am not a doctor or anything. The only way I know two people can share DNA is if they were identical twins, but I know my wife and her sister are not twins. However, when Laney was eleven and Susan was ten, Susan had leukemia. Laney donated bone marrow to save her sister. Could that explain having the same blood?"

"It sounds plausible. I will ask the forensics lab. Thank you for all your help. We identified two of the three bodies found in the basement because of your information. Unfortunately, they were your sister-in-law's ex-husbands. We just don't know who the female is."

"Wow. So when are you issuing a BOLO for my sister-in-law?"

"It is being issued as we speak."

"And I am free to go?"

"Yes, you are free to go and pick up your wife. I believe they will release her."

"Thank you, sir. Please keep me informed if you catch Susan. I am afraid for my life and my wife's."

"I will. Good luck. Go get your wife. I will let the authorities up there know you are on your way. Also, I will let them know about your theory."

As I left the police station, I had a sense of relief wash over me. Laney would be free, but now we had to live our lives worried about the revenge of her sister.

CHAPTER TWENTY-SEVEN

KARMA CATCHES UP

I couldn't believe I got myself into this predicament. I didn't even know the name of my captor. It seemed to be morning, however, with no window in the room or clock. It was hard to tell. As I sat on the edge of the bed contemplating my next move, I heard footsteps coming towards the door. The lock on the door clicked open, and the doorknob turned. The man in the green ball cap appeared with a tray of food.

"Good morning, little sister. I hope you slept well last night. I made you your favorite breakfast. I am so glad you have returned home."

This man was clearly delusional. I wasn't his sister. What was his game? I thought it best to play along until I figured out a way to get out of there.

"Good morning, bro. I slept as well as expected. This is a surprise that we found each other again."

"Why is it such a surprise? You return every year for your birthday."

The man looked at me, puzzled. Something about his facial features was oddly familiar now that I was staring at him.

"Oh, yeah, I am sorry. I forgot."

"It's all that drinking and drugs you do. It rots your mind and makes you forget so much. Maybe this year will be the year you kick the habit for good."

"I have kicked those nasty habits. Is that why you lock me in this room? To help me detox?"

His face hardened. I had unexpectedly hit a nerve.

"No, you know why you are locked in here. Eat your breakfast. I will return with your lunch when it is time."

Well, that didn't end well. Instead of figuring out why I was here, I pissed off my captor. Although I didn't quite understand why this man would lock his own sister into a room. Maybe he had a terrible relationship with her, like Laney and I had. The silence of the house was deafening. Until I heard the ringing of a telephone in the distance. It sounded as if it was coming from the room below. I scooted off the bed and put my ear on the floor to hear anything I could. I heard the voice of the man in the green cap.

"Yes, sir, this is Mark McMillan."

There was silence. Then he spoke again.

"Thank you. Yes, I can leave here right away. I can't believe you might have finally found her! She has been missing for so long."

More silence. Now my brain was filling up with questions that I had no answers for. *Where was my captor going? How long would he be gone?*

Would he leave me food? Who was she that had been found? Another captive that had gotten free?

"Yes, I have her old hairbrush in a shoebox. And I have a copy of her dental records I had gotten when she first went missing."

Dental records? Why would he have records from someone he captured, like me? The hairbrush could have been a souvenir. And then it hit me. He was going to be identifying a body. Was it the body of someone he had killed? Oh, the irony of the little joke I had made the night before in his truck struck me head-on.

"Yes, sir, her name was Melissa Macmillan. Missy for short. She was my little sister. I will be on my way."

Missy. Oh, no. No way this was happening. I was being held captive by Missy's brother. The same woman I had killed several decades ago for screwing my husband. I needed to get out of here before he found out who I was. My heart raced as I heard the footsteps coming toward the door again. This time he shoved open the door and for a fleeting moment, I thought of trying to run past him.

"I don't know who you are or why you were pretending to be my sister. She is dead. I don't have time to take care of you right now. But I will be back and when I do return, I will decide what to do with you."

"What do you mean? You called me your sister first. I just played along. You have me locked in this room. What am I supposed to do?"

His eyes glazed over, and he left the room, locking the door behind him. I was in danger. If he went and identified his sister's body, that meant they found her in the cabin. That meant they were probably piecing together all of my crimes. But it was clear I wasn't the first woman he had locked in here. Maybe using his potential crimes against him would help get me free from here. I needed to gain his trust. There was one universal way to gain a man's trust in my mind. I would have to use my womanly wiles. While he was gone, I took a shower and freshened myself up.

It felt like an eternity before he returned. My stomach growled from hunger. The toast and eggs from the morning had done little to tie me over until my next meal. Whenever that would be. There wasn't much to do in the small bedroom he confined me in. I opened the drawer of the bedside table and found a book, *Family Ties The Lyons Garden*. It had been ages since I actually read one. Reading was more Laney's thing, not mine, but since there wasn't much else to do, I cracked open the spine and started reading.

I had become immersed in the story's plot and hadn't realized my captor had returned until I heard the telltale sounds of his boots on the stairs. The footsteps stopped outside the bedroom door. It seemed like forever before I heard the click of the lock unlocking and saw the doorknob turning. When he stepped into the room, there was a mixture of rage and sadness etched onto his face.

"You! I can't believe the actual luck I had in picking you up last night. The person responsible for killing my own dear sister."

As he spoke, he stepped closer to me, where I was lying on the bed. I bolted upright and hugged my knees to my chest. I had to think fast, or I felt I was a goner.

"What are you talking about?"

"My sister Missy. You killed her!"

"Missy? You have it all wrong. I didn't kill Missy. I killed my husband, Paul. Missy was my friend, and he killed her. I killed him for revenge. I am sorry I didn't go to the police and tell them about Missy, but I was afraid they would throw me in jail. You understand revenge killing, don't you? It's what you wanted to do to me. It's what you have done to the other girls you have brought here. Right?"

As he listened to my words, I choked out some tears to help make my story more believable. His face registered a look of confusion, and the rage seemed to dissipate. When he reached the bed,

I was on, he sat on the edge. He put his head in his hands and cried.

"The police are looking for you. They say you killed her and five other men."

"So why didn't you bring them here to arrest me?"

He lifted his head and looked at me. His eyes were cold and stared deep into my own.

"I wanted to kill you myself."

"And you didn't want them finding out your secrets, right?"

"How do you know my secrets?"

I inched closer to him. My mouth was within inches of his ear.

"This room clearly has had occupants before. You are not in jail, so that means those that have stayed here before are no longer alive to tell."

I backed away and looked straight into his eyes again.

"You are pretty smart. How do I know you are telling the truth about not killing my sister?"

"Because I have nothing to lose or gain. There is nowhere for me to go. You are going to kill me or turn me over to the police. I have no future. It all ends here in this room."

"So, if I don't kill you and I let you hide out here. As a thank you for killing the bastard that killed my sister, will you keep my secrets?"

"You have yourself a deal. You let me live and I will keep your secrets."

"It's a deal then, and by the way. My name is Mark."

"Mine is Susan."

CHAPTER TWENTY-EIGHT

FREEDOM

I had lost track of the days. Being incarcerated in a foreign country was scary. My lawyer was doing everything he could to get me out. They were going to extradite me to Maine to be arraigned for the murder of Arnold. My last contact with my husband had perplexed me. LeeAnn and Cora Lynn hadn't been to visit me, but I didn't even know if I could have visitors.

I think I was in the middle of a daydream when a deputy came to get me out of my cell. Maybe they were finally going to extradite me? I didn't know.

"Mrs. Wilson, your lawyer is here to see you."

He ushered me out of the cell without hand-cuffing me, which I thought was odd. When we entered the interrogation room, my lawyer sat there, along with the two detectives in charge of my case. They all stood up as I entered and my lawyer pulled out a chair for me to sit in. As I sat down, Detective Banks sat down across from me.

"Mrs. Wilson, we are letting you go today. Recent evidence has arisen, which has made the case against you very difficult to prove."

"Are you serious? I am free?"

I looked at my lawyer, who just smiled and shook his head yes.

"But how? I thought you had DNA evidence linking me to the crime, and that made it almost open and shut."

"We do have DNA evidence, however, we were not aware of a rare medical complication in which a bone marrow recipient can carry the same DNA in their blood as the donor."

"Hold on, are you saying my sister is the one that murdered Arnold?"

"Yes, we now believe your sister Susan not only killed Arnold, Daniel, and Troy, but she also killed three other people."

"But how?"

"Well, if it wasn't for your husband, we might never have known. It appears she was pretending to be you. They went to a cabin in New Hampshire where he handcuffed her so he could get authorities after she had confessed to him. Only while he was gone, she had escaped. When she did, she left blood on the sheets. That blood was a match for you and the other cases."

"Wait, my husband, knew it wasn't me?"

"Yes. As soon as he knew you were alive and safe, he played along with her charade until he could figure out a way to clear you. He has been in contact with your friends the entire time. They have been keeping your lawyer informed."

"So, is my sister in custody?"

"No, there is an APB out for her arrest. She is considered armed and dangerous."

"That isn't comforting. How am I going to feel safe with my sister out there, knowing she had

tried to frame me for murder and take my identity?"

"I am sorry. The US authorities are doing everything they can to track her down. They have her
picture plastered all over the news. She won't be
able to hide for long."

The detectives stood up and opened the door
to the interrogation room.

"You are free to go."

At that moment, the weight of the world came
crashing down upon me. I could not contain the
emotions I was feeling, and I shook as I sobbed.
I was free. Prison was not in my future. But
the thought of having to look over my shoulder
watching for my sister terrified me. All I wanted
at that moment was to see my husband, Scott.

As if a fairy godmother had heard my wish, my
husband walked through the door of the interrogation room. He helped me stand out of my
chair and he enveloped me in his waiting arms.

"Laney, I am so sorry I had to pretend I didn't
know it was you calling. I hope you can forgive
me."

"Are you kidding me? You are my hero. If you hadn't done what you did, I would still be sitting in a jail cell. I am thankful you are alive and well."

"Let's go home. I already called your parents. They are aware of everything. The authorities have told them that if Susan contacts them, they need to call them immediately."

"What about the girls? Do they know?"

"Yes, and they can't wait to see us safe at home."

When we got out into the parking lot, LeeAnn and Cora Lynn were waiting for us. They both gave me a big hug. Then we all headed back home to Connecticut in separate vehicles. On the drive home, Scott explained how my sister attempted to steal my identity and life. Some details were unnerving. Especially when it came to my sister wanting to have sex with my husband. That opened up the old wounds that had created the divide in our sibling relationship in the first place.

I trusted my husband, and I believed him when he said he did nothing with her, but that tiny sliver of doubt sat in the back of my mind. Just the thought of my sister lying naked in front of him turned my stomach. I just didn't understand what went wrong with my sister. Her mindset was so completely twisted. From what we had learned about her in the last few days, she had apparently lost touch with reality a long time ago. Long before our relationship ended. My sister was a killer, a serial killer at that. She had become one at the young age of fifteen.

We grew up in the same household. The two of us went to the same schools. I always felt my parents treated her a little more lenient, especially after the leukemia diagnosis. That certainly couldn't have caused her to become a psychopath. She did always crave attention, though. I closed my eyes and drifted off to sleep, still contemplating what turned my sister into a monster.

CHAPTER TWENTY-NINE

NEW LIFE

Mark seemed to believe my story that I didn't kill his sister, which was a blessing for me. If he hadn't believed me, I would have ended up dead or in prison. Instead, Mark and I learned to live with each other. It took a lot of trust-building between the two of us. We knew each other's darkest secrets. And we both knew we could use those secrets against each other at any moment. It took him months before he stopped locking me in the upstairs bedroom. Even when he locked me up there, he still brought me three hot home-cooked meals a day and sat with me while I ate.

This had given us time to get to know each other. In some strange way, I found him fascinating. The death of his sister had sent him into a spiral of despair. The authorities hadn't taken his pleas to search for her seriously because she had been a chronic runaway and drug user. They felt she had just run away again. Every year around the time of her birthday, he would make another attempt to convince the authorities to search for her. Failing every time. Then he would find a woman to act as a surrogate sister and would bring her home to the locked bedroom.

He locked her in to prevent her from running away again. No matter how well he treated her, though, the woman would eventually anger him. At the moment, he would lash out. Unfortunately, for the many women this happened to, the outcome was always the same. He wound up killing them.

We were kindred spirits. Being with him almost made me forget my hatred for my sister and her husband. Almost. I wanted revenge. She was free, as always, to live her perfect life. While I was grateful to be alive, I would never again live absolutely carefree. I had made it to the FBI's most wanted list. The cabin and the surrounding woods had become my world.

As I walked my usual daily path through the woods and back to the cabin, I contemplated how I could exact my revenge on my sister. I would need Mark's assistance, but I wasn't sure he would be willing to help. He was chopping wood when I approached the cabin. He must have seen me coming because he stopped mid-swing and smiled at me.

"How was your walk?"

"It was peaceful, as always. A bit lonely. Maybe tomorrow you will want to join me?"

"I will consider it. There is a stew made on the stove. I was waiting for you to return so we could have lunch together."

"Thank you. I did work up an appetite with my walk."

We went into the cabin and he pulled out a chair for me at the dining room table. It surprised me how gentlemanly he always was. For a man who was a cold-blooded serial killer, like me, his manners always shocked me. In the months that I had been with him, he never once laid a finger on me. Not that I wouldn't have minded his touch in an affectionate way. I often wondered if he was even into women sexually or not. He had the freedom to date whomever he wanted, unlike me, whose only option for the foreseeable future would be him. Yet, he chose not to. Today seemed like a good time to find out one way or another. I personally had never gone this long without having sex and I was feeling frisky at the moment.

"Do you find me attractive?"

Mark looked at me as I asked him the question. He was in the middle of ladling out some stew into the bowl he had placed in front of me.

"Of course, I find you attractive. I would have to be blind or stupid not to."

He finished ladling the stew and sat down across from me.

"Then how come this entire time I have been here you haven't put a single move on me?"

"No offense, but you have told me why you killed all those other men. Each one of them you had sex with. I prefer to live."

This took me by surprise. I guess I never really thought about that little fact about myself and the men I murdered. It could be intimidating to have a sexual relationship with a woman who killed some men she had relations with.

"Well, just for the record. I didn't kill every man I had sex with."

He looked up at me with raised eyebrows as he brought a spoonful of stew to his mouth.

"Is that so? Maybe I will have to reconsider my no-touch stance with you. Unless, of course, you do not want me to."

"If I didn't want you to, I wouldn't have asked you if you found me attractive."

I slid my foot under the table, up his leg to his thigh. As I did, he almost choked on the mouthful of stew.

"See, you almost killed me."

He laughed as he wiped his mouth with a napkin.

"I wouldn't let you die. I can give you mouth-to-mouth resuscitation."

Pushing back my chair and standing up. His eyes followed my every move as I came around to his side of the table. Placing my right hand under his chin, and gently turned his face towards mine. Then I bent down and met his lips with mine. He wasn't lying about his attraction to me because there was absolutely no resistance. He met the intensity I kissed him with, with his own fiery passion. That night I found myself wrapped up in his bedsheets for the first of many times. It was the start of the most beautiful relationship I had ever experienced.

Chapter Thirty

WAITING

Scott and I were relieved when we returned home from that crazy trip. Our girls and my parents were anxiously waiting for us. The next six months were nerve-racking for us all. We were constantly looking over our shoulders, waiting for my sister to show up. We both went through counseling to help us deal with the post-traumatic stress we experienced during the entire ordeal.

I insisted we get our pistol permits to protect ourselves. That was a process in itself. The NRA gun safety course was the first step. My accuracy impressed the instructor for the first time shooting a gun.

"I wouldn't piss off your wife, Mr. Wilson. She is pretty good at this."

My husband raised his eyebrows as he watched me hit the target in a perfect cluster in the center of the bullseye.

"I will try to remember that."

Then came the paperwork and fingerprinting. And finally came the waiting for the background checks and the paperwork to be processed. I felt like my entire purpose in life was waiting. Waiting for my sister to show her evilness. Waiting to get the permit to protect myself from her craziness. The weight of knowing she was out there and capable of killing us was like a black cloud of death following us everywhere we went.

Every time the news reported a woman's body found anywhere in the United States, I secretly wished it would be her, so we could stop being afraid. That made me feel like a monster. *How could I wish my sister was dead?* My therapist said it was a normal trauma response. That still didn't make me feel any less of a savage.

It was only after a full year had passed that I believed she would never show up. I didn't think she had that much self-control, so I thought the worst had happened to her. It was my forty-seventh birthday, and I had just retrieved the mail from the mailbox. As I sifted through the bills and several cards from friends and relatives, one stood out. I didn't recognize the handwriting. There was no return address. When I checked the postmark, it had come from California. I didn't know anyone from there. My stomach dropped. I didn't want to open it, but a part of me was curious. I left it on the counter and I called my husband. His voice always had a calming effect on me.

"Hey Baby, how is the birthday girl doing?"

"I was doing well until I went to the mailbox. Do we know anyone in California?"

"Not that I can recall. Why?"

"I received what appears to be a card with no return address, but they postmarked it from California."

"Did you open it?"

"No, should I?"

"I think you should call the police and let them handle it."

"You don't think it's from Susan, do you?"

"Babe, it might be. We should err on the side of caution."

"Okay, I will call."

"Do you want me to come home?"

"Would you please?"

"Sure thing, I will be there shortly."

While I waited for Scott to get home, I called the police. They were aware of my situation, so they said they would send a unit right over. I didn't realize they were going to send a bomb squad. After they determined there was probably nothing dangerous in the letter, they opened it. It was a handmade birthday card made of cut and pasted letters. It said, "Happy Birthday, enjoy your day because it will be your last."

There was no signature, but I knew who it was from. She had lulled me into a sense of security and chose my birthday to shake me out of it. Scott held me as I cried. The police called in the

FBI and they started an investigation to track her down. The postmark was from California, however, that was days prior. She may not even be there now.

Over the next few weeks, I received more taunting letters from my sister. Each one made the same as the first one. None with a return address. She postmarked them all from different places. It would seem as if she were crossing the country, coming toward me, and then she would backtrack to another state farther away. The mind games were working.

I was an anxious mess. Sleep had become something of an enigma. We had sent our daughters to live with friends during their college breaks to keep them safe. Then, just as suddenly as the letters had started, they stopped. She had postmarked the last one from Kentucky. It was closer than California, but still far enough away for us to think she might not make it back to Connecticut.

The constant stress was taking a toll on my health. Especially my mental health. There were days I contemplated ending my life. My thought process was if I was gone, my sister would leave my family alone. The therapist helped me understand my sister wouldn't stop torturing them if I was gone. Psychopaths keep going until someone else stops them.

That didn't make me feel better, but at least I no longer wanted to kill myself. I joined a gym and trained. As my body got stronger, my mindset grew as well. I figured if my sister came for me, I would be as prepared as I could be to fight her off. That is, if she actually came for me. She very well could just play mind games for the rest of our lives and torture me that way.

I hated the waiting. Not knowing when or where she would show up. It was enough to drive a person clinically insane. The authorities had no leads on her whereabouts. Throughout the investigation of the letters, there were no sightings of her anywhere.

CHAPTER THIRTY-ONE

TRAVELING AROUND

Mark quickly fell in love with me, so when I begged him to buy a motorhome so we could travel around, he didn't hesitate. The four walls of the cabin were closing in on me. It was easy for me to stay out of sight in most places, traveling in the camper. I just didn't get out of the RV. It was invigorating being able to go all over the country and not worry about getting caught.

When we were in California, I realized my sister's birthday was coming up.

"Honey, can you help me with a minor project?"

"Sure. What do you need me to do?"

"I need you to pick up these items on this list."

Mark looked at the list and then looked at me with one eyebrow raised.

"I want to send my dear older sister a birthday card."

I smiled sweetly at him. He chuckled.

"Whatever you want."

He wasn't gone long. The supplies weren't much. I donned a pair of gloves so I wouldn't leave any fingerprints, although I am sure she would figure out who it was from. When it was ready to be mailed out, I had him drop it off in a postal box. I was giddy with excitement at imagining her reaction.

We didn't stay in any single place for long and I made a game out of sending more letters out. I wanted her to be terrified. Her perfect life needed to be ruined. I couldn't really be free, so I didn't want her to be free either. I wanted her to fear me for the rest of her life. Which, if I had my way, would not be long at all.

But I wasn't sure Mark would be up for more murders. He seemed content with the life we had built. The letters didn't bother him much because we were careful not to leave traces that could lead to us. In my mind, my sister and her husband needed to go. Especially Scott. It was because of him, after all, that my sister was free and I had to go into hiding.

As we trekked back towards New England and our home in Vermont, the desire to see my sister grew stronger. I stopped sending her letters when we hit Kentucky. I wanted to sneak up on her, lull her into a sense of security, then pop up when she least expected it. My plans needed to be secret. I didn't want to involve Mark. So I kept my thoughts to myself.

"We need to head home to Vermont. It's almost Missy's birthday and I need to be there to celebrate with her."

I had my back turned to Mark when he said this to me. This made it easy for me to conceal the rolling of my eyes. Missy was dead. Long gone, his need to celebrate her birthday with her annoyed me. All he would do was go to her grave with some flowers, sit there and pretend to talk to her. It wasn't like she could respond to him. I had hoped our time on the road, away from her grave, would have cured him of his obsession with visiting her. Apparently, it hadn't.

"Whatever you need, dear. But before we head home, can we make a stop in Connecticut?"

As I said this, I walked over to where he was sitting on the RV couch and straddled his lap. I knew how to persuade him to do the things I wanted to do.

"Babe, it's not safe for us to go to Connecticut. Whatever would make you want to even consider it?"

"Well, all this talk of your sister. It makes me miss mine. Maybe if I can see her in person, I can explain everything to her. I can explain that I killed those guys in self-defense."

I pouted, putting my head on his shoulder while looking up at him with sad puppy dog eyes.

"You really think she will listen to you?"

"I am her kid sister. She gave me her bone marrow to save my life. I know deep down she still cares about me. We have had a really rocky past, I admit it. I caused most of it, but I think she can forgive me if I prove to her I have changed."

"You aren't afraid she will call the cops on you?"

"I will do what I can to minimize that risk."

"Babe, I don't like it. I think it is too risky. What happens if she calls the police, and you get arrested? You will go to jail for life, or worse."

"She won't. I want to see my sister. Why can't you understand that?"

"I understand. You know I do. I don't want to lose you, though."

"You won't ever lose me."

"Can I go with you? Just to make sure you stay safe?"

"No! I need you to stay in the RV and stay out of sight. There is a park down the road from her house. You can park there. I will walk from there. It is close enough that if I need to make a quick getaway, I can."

"I don't like it. What if her husband is there?"

"He won't be. I won't go when he is home."

I lied through my teeth. The goal was to have both of them at home. I wanted them both dead.

"How will you know if he is home or not?"

"If his truck isn't in the driveway, that means he is at work for his shift."

"It could be in the garage."

"He doesn't leave it in the garage. He is a firefighter, he doesn't enjoy putting his vehicle in the garage. It is one of his weird oddities."

"If you are sure? I guess we can stop briefly on our way home."

"Thanks, babe, I love you!"

"I love you too. I would do anything for you. You know that, right?"

"Yes, I do."

Of course, I knew that. I had trained him well. I always met his needs.

Chapter Thirty-Two

SURPRISE VISITORS

Thanksgiving break was coming up. Our girls really wanted to come home for the holiday. I was feeling nervous about allowing them to come home. I had not received any more letters, but we still had no clues about the location of Susan. The last thing we knew, she was in Kentucky. She had postmarked the last letter from there. That had been months ago. I wanted desperately to have my girls back home under our roof once again. As a mom, not being able to see them come and go as they pleased, without restriction, hurt my heart.

The anger towards my sister deepened every day. Scott and I seemed to grow apart. We were still in counseling, but he seemed to feel we needed to move on with our lives and not let Susan dictate what we did or didn't do. I knew deep down he was right. Prior to learning about the atrocities she had committed, I didn't care about her or worry about her. Now, though, knowing how evil she had become and what she was capable of doing sent shivers up my spine every time I thought about her. I couldn't move on. The thought of her out there paralyzed me to my very core.

My phone rang. It was Makayla, our oldest daughter.

"Hey sweetie, I am so glad you called. I was missing you and your sisters."

"You know, Mom, that can easily be rectified. You can allow us to come home for Thanksgiving break."

"It's not that simple Kay, you know that. What if Aunt Susan shows up?"

"Mom, it's been over a year now. I think the coast is clear."

"I am not so sure of that. And until I am, I don't want you girls in harm's way."

"When do you think the coast will be clear, Mom? A week, a month, a year, ten years? Are you going to let your sister control your life forever?"

"I don't know when the coast will be clear. I just can't imagine anything happening to you or your sisters. It would break me."

"Well, we have decided we are done staying away from you and Dad. We are coming home this weekend. All three of us. Dad knows, and he has agreed. Living in fear is not living."

The tears welled up in my eyes. My heart raced. The phone in my hand almost slipped out because of how sweaty it had become.

"No, no. You guys can't do this. What if she is watching and waiting?"

"Let her mom. You and Dad have your pistol permits. We have all taken self-defense classes. We are done living in fear."

My body shook. Of course, she was right. That didn't change the terror I felt in my bones.

"I can't change your mind. Can I?"

"Nope. We need this. You and Dad need this. We aren't blind to what is happening there at home. We know the strain this is causing in your relationship. Maybe with us being all together, it will help mend things."

"And what if it doesn't mend things? What if it is beyond repair?"

"Then we will handle that as a family, Mom. You can't do this on your own."

Everything she was saying was true. How did my daughter get wiser than me? And braver?

"I guess I don't have a choice in this, do I?"

"Nope. We will be home on Saturday."

We said our goodbyes and ended our call. I sat on the couch, wrapping my arms around myself, and sobbed. I didn't know how to let go of the fear. Nothing I had done had helped ease it. I was home alone again. Scott had been taking more overtime shifts at work. He said it was to make up for me not working anymore. I had given up my job because it became too much for me. Scott, working so much, felt more like he was avoiding me and the distance that was forming between us. Maybe Makayla was right. I needed to stop living in fear of my sister and just live.

If the girls were coming home for the weekend, I needed to make sure their rooms were fresh for them. I pulled myself together and went upstairs to prep their rooms. As I worked to tidy things up, I felt a renewed sense of life. It had been so long since we spent time together as a family. It was dark outside, and the wind howled. There was a storm brewing. Thankfully, it wasn't a nor'easter. With a gust of wind, the window to my daughter Mackenzie's room rattled and made me jump. When I looked up and realized it was just the wind, I strode over to the window to pull down the blinds.

There were headlights driving slowly down our road. They slowed as they approached the house and the hair on the back of my neck rose. The vehicle stopped briefly in front of the house. It was an RV. The engine revved, and it drove off.

I shook my head. *Stop living in fear.* I hated how jumpy I had become. My confidence in myself had diminished to only a shadow of what it once was. I put on some music to get my mind off the RV and the brewing storm. Soon I was dancing from one room to the other, straightening up and prepping for my girl's return home. It was ten o'clock when I had finished. My cell phone rang. It was Scott.

"Hey Babe, just calling to say goodnight. We have been running all evening to various calls."

"Oh, I didn't even realize how late it was. I got a phone call from Makayla today, but I am sure you are aware of that since you told the girls it was okay to come home. I have been prepping their rooms for them."

I tried to hide the bitterness in my voice, but he picked up on it.

"Look, I know you are still in fear mode. I am sorry that you are having trouble moving past what your sister did. We are moving on."

"That's great that you all can move on. I am sorry I can't. I am trying, really I am."

I debated telling him about the RV that had driven by, but if I told him, it would just affirm his belief that I wasn't trying to move on. I wouldn't give him that satisfaction.

"Laney, I know you are trying, but you need to try harder. I love you, you know that, and I hate seeing you like this."

"How am I supposed to try harder? What more can I do? I can't help the way I feel, Scott."

"I have to go. The tones are going off. I love you. Goodnight."

"Love you too. Be safe."

CHAPTER THIRTY-THREE

THE STOP

We drove slowly past my sister's house. As I looked up at the room with the light on, I saw her clear as day. She was watching us. Mark realized she was watching and accidentally revved the engine as he sped up to drive away.

"I hope she didn't notice us."

"Well, she was looking out the window and you revved the engine, so I am sure she noticed something. Hopefully, she doesn't call the cops or anything."

"Sorry, it startled me seeing her watching. My foot slipped."

"It's okay. Just drive down the road to the park. We can see the house from there with the binoculars. We will watch and see if the cops get called."

We parked in the park parking lot, and we watched and waited. The wind whipped as the rain pelted the roof of the RV. No cops showed, which gave me the impression the coast was clear. I gathered my rain gear.

"Why are you getting ready to go outside?"

"I am going to walk to her house and pay her a visit."

"In the rain? This late at night?"

"Mark, honey. I am a wanted woman. The rain storm and darkness give me some protection against being seen."

"Let me go with you, please."

"No. I need to do this myself. You must promise me you will stay here. If you see any cops go to the house, leave."

"But I don't want you to get caught!"

"Look, if I get caught, you are in danger. I will do my best to stay safe. If things go awry and I don't get caught, I will catch up with you. Please don't worry."

I opened the door to the RV and a gust of wind almost took the door from my hand. As I slammed the door shut behind me, I pulled the hood of my raincoat up and over my head. I bent into the wind and the rain as I walked to my sister's house. The house that was almost mine. Her life could have been mine. If her husband hadn't messed up my plans.

The walk to Laney's house wasn't long from the park. There were no lights on, which gave me the illusion my sister was probably in bed sleeping. I crept around to the back of the house. When I put my hand on the door handle to the French doors leading to the back deck, it wouldn't budge. There had to be another way I could get inside. As I searched in the darkness and rain, I tried every window with no luck. Then I remembered the garage had a door on the side of it. Sloshing through the rain to the side of the garage, I jumped at a tremendous clap of thunder and a flash of lightning. The lightning lit up the neighborhood, and I briefly worried someone would see me. Then I realized it had gotten darker. The power had gone out to the neighborhood. This made me smile.

I reached for the door handle and turned it. It was unlocked, so I pushed and went inside the garage. By this time, every inch of my body was cold and wet despite wearing a raincoat, which annoyed me. I used the mini flashlight I had brought to illuminate my path. Scott kept their garage tidy, and for this I was thankful. Only Laney's car was in the garage. Even though I wanted to exact my revenge on Scott as well, I had to commit to just taking care of my sister. Losing her would be torture enough for him.

It was quiet in the dark, and I moved slowly to keep the peace and avoid detection. The door to the house was unlocked as well, and I slowly opened it. I paused, listening for any sign of movement within the house. As I closed the door, it made a slight creaking noise that made me stop in my tracks. After a few minutes and no sound from my sister, I crept through the house. I made my way upstairs to the master bedroom. The bedroom I had shared with my sister's husband for a few days. Oh, how I wished I was able to consummate that relationship with him. That was a big regret of mine. I stood outside the closed door with my ear pressed against it. There was no noise from behind the door. My hand felt the metal of the doorknob in its grip. Slowly, I turned it and pushed the door open.

It was pitch dark in the room. Another clap of thunder rattled the house and the flash of lightning lit up the room enough for a brief second for me to see my sister. She was there, not sleeping. Instead, she was sitting on her bed with her back against her headboard. There was something in her hand, but the darkness returned before I could figure out what it was. I didn't expect her to be awake, let alone sitting there as if she was waiting for me. My mind raced. I stared at the darkness and let my eyes adjust. She sat there, not saying a word.

Lightning flashed again, and I focused my eyes on what my sister had in her hands. To my horror, I realized she had a gun. The darkness returned, and I contemplated turning and running.

Then it occurred to me, she hadn't shot at me yet. Why hadn't she? Maybe I could disarm her somehow?

"Hi, Laney. I am so glad you are awake."

"Why? So I can be conscious of who killed me? I know why you are here, Susan. I just don't know why it took you so long."

"Kill you? Why would I do that to my loving, kind sister who saved my life?"

"Yes, I saved your life years ago. That naïve little girl is gone, sis. I hold your future in my hands at the moment. I am not afraid to pull the trigger and end this once and for all."

She was right. The cards were in her hands. I never played poker with my sister, but I know she used to play with her friends on the weekends in high school and came home every time with more money than she left. Some would call her facial expression a resting bitch face. I had always called it the perfect poker face. There was never any way to tell what Laney was thinking. This was still the case. I tried listening to her voice since it was still dark and I could not see her clearly. There was no quivering. Not a single waver in her tone led me to believe she meant every word she said.

CHAPTER THIRTY-FOUR

NO MORE WAITING

My gut instinct told me it was Susan in the RV. I didn't call the cops. Instead, I peered out at the RV periodically as I prepared for my daughters to return home and waited as the storm outside raged on. I didn't even tell Scott when he called. Whatever would happen tonight would be between me and my sister. I made sure all the lights were off after hanging up with Scott to make her think I had gone to bed. I locked every door and window to the house, except the garage door on the side. Every couple of minutes, I would look down the road, hoping to see the moment she headed my way. When I saw the dark figure exit the RV and head toward my house, I went upstairs to my bedroom and waited.

It seemed like an eternity. I must have counted to one hundred a billion times as I sat quietly in my bed. The calmness I felt, though, was oddly refreshing after living in fear for over a year. Whatever happened tonight, I knew in my heart, it would all end. Here and now. My sister might have thought she was quiet, but I heard her on the deck. It was a few minutes later I heard the door between the garage and the house creaking. Thank god Scott hadn't fixed that yet. I heard her creep through the house.

Years of being a mom had trained my hearing for the slightest sounds. It was perfect timing when she opened the door to my bedroom at the same time as the thunder and lightning. The look of shock on her face seeing me sitting there was priceless. It wasn't until the second flash of lightning that it registered that I was holding a gun in my hands. The look of horror would have been comical if we weren't in a unique situation. But it wasn't funny. My sister was here to kill me, and I was fully prepared to take her life if I needed to.

She spoke to me and I could tell by the quiver in her voice I had caught her off guard. I clarified I was in control. It took her a few minutes to regain her composure. She never moved from the doorway where she stood. Whenever the lightning flashed, I could see the fear in her eyes. A minor part of me felt bad for her. The younger version of me who would have done everything in her power to protect her little sister. The version of me who endured the extraction of my bone marrow to donate to her. To save her life. Now the older, wiser, tired-of-being-used version of me was done. I could pull the trigger and it would all be over. Nobody would blame me. She had framed me for the murders of three men and had tried to take over my life while I was being held in custody. I needed answers first, though.

"Why Susan? Why did you kill those men?"

"Men? You mean boys, Laney. They were boys. All out for one thing and one thing only. They didn't want love or relationships. All they wanted was sex. They used me. So I killed them so no other girl would feel the way I did."

"Susan, you killed them because you had sex with them, thinking they would have a relationship with you? That's crazy! The entire week we were in Canada, you flirted with Arnold. You flashed him for god's sake. You snuck out of the house to meet up with him. We lived in Connecticut and he lived there. How could you have possibly thought he wanted a relationship?"

"I was fifteen, Laney. I wasn't thinking about distance and logistics. The fact was I liked him a lot, and of course he liked you."

"That was not my fault. I can't help who likes me and who doesn't. But why did you set me up to take the fall for the murders?"

"I didn't. Well, not on purpose anyway. Had I known it was the blood that connected me and you to the murders, I wouldn't have left any at my cabin on the sheets. Then you would still be in jail for those murders. I only left the blood to get Scott arrested and keep the cops off my trail."

"So you didn't purposely leave blood at the crime scenes?"

"When you called Scott and said there was DNA evidence linking you to all three murders, I didn't know it was blood. I just tipped off the Canadian authorities that you would be in the area again and you were the last person to see Arnold alive."

"But I wasn't, you were."

"I went out dressed, looking like you. And as far as Arnold knew at first, I was you, so he wouldn't have told anyone I was with him."

"How did you find out it was the blood then?"

"That is the ironic thing. Well, when Scott led the police to my cabin, and they found the blood, they, of course, investigated things further. One thing led to another, and they found the bodies in the basement."

"Yeah, I know about the bodies. That doesn't explain how you found out it was the blood that linked you to the murders I was being held for."

"Oh, Mark told me that. When the police contacted him about his sister's body, they told him I was their prime suspect and to be on the lookout for me."

I was more confused than ever. I did not know who Mark was. The storm raged on as we talked and the flashes of lightning helped me keep trained on my sister. She hadn't moved, but now and then, it seemed as if there were slight shadows of movement behind her. It had to be the eery lighting from the lightning though, because no one knew we were having the conversation we were having. Not the cops, nor Scott.

"Wait, who is Mark?"

Susan laughed. It was a big belly laugh, too.

"Oh Mark, at first I thought he was my demise. Turns out he has been my savior."

"What? That makes no sense."

"When I escaped, Mark picked me up hitchhiking and brought me to his home. He locked me in a room and I had no way to escape."

"He locked you in a room? That doesn't sound like a savior. That sounds like a psychopath."

"Oh, he is that, too. When his little sister Missy went missing, he lost his mind. The police wouldn't even look for her because she was an adult, an addict, and had been a habitual runaway."

"Wait, wasn't that the name of the girl whose remains they found in the basement of your cabin?"

She cackled.

"That's the one! It seems that he would pick up women every year around her birthday and lock them in the room. He would pretend they were his sister and celebrate with them. Then he would snap out of it and get angry with them for pretending to be his sister."

"That's certifiable insanity. What did he do to them when he realized they weren't her?"

"He killed them."

"Oh my god, Susan. He is a serial killer, just like you! How can he be your savior? Why didn't he kill you when he found out that you killed his sister?"

"He didn't kill me because I lied to him. I told him Paul had killed Missy, and she had been my best friend, so I killed Paul. The truth is, I killed them both. She was a whore, and she was sleeping with my husband. They both got what they deserved."

I gasped as another clap of thunder boomed, and the flash of lightning illuminated the room. In that instant, I saw a figure behind my sister raise its arm and then lower it. My sister screamed from the surprise and the pain. As she fell to the ground, the figure followed her and continued to strike her.

"You lying bitch!"

It was a man's voice, and I assumed this was Mark. I knew he was just as dangerous as my sister. He had to have heard our conversation. I knew what he was. That meant he would come for me when he was done with my sister. I aimed at the noise and the shadowy movements. I pulled the trigger and fired the pistol I had almost forgotten I had been holding.

Chapter Thirty-Five

TOO LONG

The minute Susan stepped out of the RV, my heart raced. I felt as if I would never see her again. My gut rumbled and tightened. I know she wanted to do this alone. Fear gripped me, and I paced back and forth in the camper. I couldn't lose her. Losing my sister Missy had taken a huge toll on me for so long. Susan had been my saving grace. Learning she had brought justice to Missy's killer had healed my broken heart. I couldn't bear to lose her.

I grabbed my dark hooded sweatshirt, opened the door to the RV, and stepped out into the pelting rain and the driving wind. I couldn't see Susan down the block at her sister's house. The storm had knocked the neighborhood's power out. My steps hastened as I got closer to the house. I knew Susan was going to attempt to get in from the back, so that was where I started. There was no sign of her getting in, so I went around the garage and found a door there that was unlocked. I crept through to the next door and entered the house. The murmurs of voices were coming from upstairs, so I made my way up.

It was hard to see in the dark. I made my way toward what appeared to be the master bed-room. I tried to flatten myself against the wall so no one would detect me coming. With every flash of lightning, I could see Susan standing in the bedroom doorway, frozen like a statue. What was beyond her, I could not see, but I could hear another female's voice. I presumed it was her sister's. When I was about three feet from Susan, I stopped to listen to their conversation.

My heart fluttered when Susan said my name and called me her savior. I really loved her. When we got back to the RV, I would tell her how much she meant to me. I would propose. There was no one I ever wanted to spend the rest of my life with before Susan. We had crossed the country together. Both of us had deep dark secrets, we promised to keep for each other.

Then I heard her exposing my secrets to her sister, and my heart sank. *Why was she telling her?* I reached into my pocket and pulled out my pocketknife. As I opened it to expose the blade, I realized it had been so long since I had used my old friend. Maybe Susan had a reason for telling her sister my secret. It wouldn't matter if Susan was planning on killing her. That had to be it. She was toying with her, scaring her, as she did with the letters.

It wasn't until I heard Susan cackle and then explain how she had lied to me about my sweet sister Missy, that it hit me like a two-by-four on the forehead. She had used me all this time. I held my knife tight in my grip and I lunged toward her back. The knife entered her right below her left shoulder blade. As I removed it, she screamed, falling to the floor. I fell to my knees and continued to stab her. I was oblivious to her sister, but I knew I would have to take care of her when I was done. She knew my secrets, so I couldn't let her live.

There was a loud noise. At first, I thought it was another clap of thunder, but then I felt the searing pain in my shoulder. I reached up with my other hand and felt the sticky wetness of blood. *Shit, the bitch had a gun!* I heard more shots fired and one by one they hit me. The pain increased with each wound and as I fell onto Susan's limp body, my last thought was, *Susan got her wish. Laney became a murderer just like her.*

CHAPTER THIRTY-SIX

RELIEF

I unloaded the entire clip of six bullets into the dark figure. When he collapsed onto my sister's body, I dropped the gun. My hand shook as I reached for my cell phone. As I dialed 911, my stomach rolled, and I fought the wave of nausea that was hitting me full force.

"911, what is your emergency?"

"I... um. I just shot an intruder."

"What is your name? And where are you calling from?"

"My name is Laney Wilson. I am calling from 110 Cherry Brook Lane."

"Laney, where is the intruder now?"

"He is lying on the floor, well, really lying on top of my sister, who is lying on the floor."

"Ma'am, did you say the intruder was on top of your sister?"

"Yes, he was stabbing her, and I shot him."

"Are they alive?"

"I don't know. I hope not."

"Ma'am, I am sending the police and EMS to the scene. Can you unlock the door for them?"

"No, I can't. The bodies are blocking the doorway to my bedroom."

"Okay. Is there a key outside your house that they can use to enter?"

"No, but the side door to the garage is unlocked. That's how they got in. They can enter that way."

I imagined Scott would hear the call come in and would rush to the scene. The dispatcher was friendly and helped to keep me calm. She explained she wanted to prevent me from going into shock. This was extremely helpful. It didn't take long for the police to show up and enter my house. They approached my bedroom with flashlights on and guns drawn. I hung up with the dispatcher and raised my hands over my head. I didn't want them to shoot me.

One officer stepped over the bodies while the next bent down to look for signs of life.

"Ma'am, where is the gun?"

"It is right here on the bed."

"Don't move. I am going to place you in hand-cuffs."

He approached and told me to get off the bed. I did exactly what he asked me to do. As he placed the handcuffs on my wrists, I couldn't help but think back to how this entire ordeal had started. The officer helped me navigate over the bodies as he led me to his squad car.

The fire rescue pulled up and Scott jumped out. He ran to me as the officer was helping me sit in the back.

"Laney, are you okay? What happened?"

"Scott, I think it's all over."

"Sir, she can't talk to you right now. I need to take her down to the police station. There are two victims upstairs though that need attending to."

"Laney, I love you!"

"I love you too, Scott."

The officer closed the door to the cruiser and Scott rushed into our house to tend to Mark and Susan.

The blue and red lights flashed in the darkness as the cruiser drove me to the station. The rain pelted the roof and the wipers on the windshield swished back and forth. It gave me the feeling of déjà vu. When we made it to the station, they brought me into an interrogation room. Two men in black suits entered and sat down across from me.

"Mrs. Wilson, my name is Agent Hall, and this is Agent Waters. We need to get your statement of what transpired this evening."

"Yes, I know the drill."

"Okay, so start from the beginning."

"Well, I was cleaning my daughter's room, and I noticed an RV drive by really slowly. I had a gut feeling it was my sister, Susan. I am sure you are aware of my situation with her."

"We know that we have accused her of at least six murders. So if you thought it was her, why didn't you contact us?"

"Honestly, I don't know why I didn't contact you. Maybe I wasn't one hundred percent sure it was her. Or maybe I was tired of living in fear of when she would come and try to kill me."

"Go on. What happened next?"

"I made sure I locked the windows and doors. Then I headed upstairs to my bedroom."

"Mrs. Wilson, you told dispatch that your sister and the other intruder got in from the unlocked garage door. You told them that was how they could enter the house."

"Yes, I did. My sister had told me that was how she got in. I rarely use it, and usually, that one stays locked, so I didn't check."

"Okay, so what did your sister do when she found you?"

"Nothing. We were just talking. She saw I had my gun to defend myself, so she kept her distance."

"When did the other intruder arrive?"

"I am not sure. Now that I am thinking about it, I thought I saw someone behind my sister a few times, but it was dark. At first, I thought it was just shadows playing tricks on my mind."

"When did you realize it wasn't just shadows?"

"When he started stabbing my sister and called her 'A lying bitch.'"

"So why do you think he stabbed her?"

"She had lied to him, told him she had killed her husband Paul because Paul had killed his sister Missy. Then she confessed the truth to me. She killed them both because they were having an affair. He must have heard her confession."

"So why did you shoot at him? There was obviously no love lost between you and your sister, and you thought she was going to kill you. He eliminated that threat for you."

"I shot at him because she had told me his dark secret. He was a serial killer as well. I knew deep down, he was going to come at me next."

"Wait, your sister hooked up with a serial killer and then double-crossed him?"

"Apparently. She said he went crazy after his sister went missing and every year he kidnapped and killed a woman around her birthday."

"Okay. We are going to have to hold you until we check everything out."

"Yeah, I know the process. Remember, been there, done that."

Another officer led me to a holding cell. This was definitely becoming a habit, one I hoped I could finally break free of. The other officer woke me up early the next morning, flanked by my attorney.

"Good news Laney, they won't be charging you with any crime. The DA feels you were justified in killing Mark since you had just witnessed him killing your sister and she confessed to his crimes. They searched his property and found several shallow graves. Your story panned out."

"I am free?"

"Yes, Laney, you are free."

"What about Susan and Mark?"

"They succumbed to their injuries. They are dead."

I was numb. I know I should be happy that my sister was gone. There should be a relief filling my body knowing I never had to fear for my life again. Yet, I oddly felt sad. I knew losing my sister would take its toll on my parents. Her being a fugitive wanted for murder already had. They both had aged about ten years during the time this situation unfolded. How could I face them knowing I led my sister to the slaughter? Yes, Mark had killed her that night, but if he hadn't, I was fully prepared to take her life myself.

When we made it to the lobby of the station, it surprised me to find my parents, Scott, and all three of my daughters waiting for me. They gathered around me and encircled me with the biggest hugs. Scott was the last to hug me. He squeezed so hard it was as if he never wanted to let me go again. Then he released me and put his arm around my shoulder.

"Let's go home, Laney. And by home, I mean your parent's house because I think we can agree that it is time to sell our house and start fresh."

"Absolutely!"

I would miss our old house. The one we raised our daughters in, but honestly, a fresh start sounded fantastic.

The End

ABOUT AUTHOR

A former paraeducator, novice genealogist, turned author D.M. Foley is an award-winning writer. Her first book, The Lyons Garden Book One Family Ties, received The New York Best Sellers Gold Award in December 2021. She lives in Southeastern, Ct, with her husband, three sons, and her mom. You can follow her on her social media accounts at:

D.M. Foley - Author Page on Facebook
@d.m._foley on Instagram and TikTok
@DMFoleyauthor on Twitter
Foley's Fable Followers Facebook Group
Contact Information:
d.m.foleyauthor@gmail.com

D.M. FOLEY

D.M. Foley
P.O. Box 735
54 Main Street
Jewett City, CT
06351

BOOKS BY THIS AUTHOR

Family Ties The Lyons Garden Book One
Erasing Secrets The Lyons Garden Book Two
Pawns The Lyons Garden Book Three

Deric Dream Changer Book 1 Of The Dream Walkers Series

The Killer Trip

The Immortal Lies (Coming October 2023)

Acknowledgments

Where do I start? There are so many people to thank and acknowledge for their support in my writing career.

To my husband John, thank you for your patience and understanding with this journey I have undertaken. Maybe someday I will become your sugar momma. Love you.

To my son Johnny, thank you for always giving me words of encouragement and support. Love you.

To my son Christopher, thank you for your financial advice for deciding what marketing strategies I should use. Love you.

To my son Eric, thank you for being my IT guy and helping me when I run into technical difficulties. Love you.

To my Mom, thank you for being my biggest supporter and cheerleader. Whether I am selling books or Girl Scout cookies, you have always had my back! Love you.

To my brother Keith and his wife Lisa, thank you for being supporters and reading my books. Love you.

To all my family and friends who have taken the time to read any of my books, thank you. It means the world to me to have your support. Love you.

To CP Ann and Raven, thank you for helping me moderate my private reader group, Foley's Fable Followers on Facebook, so I can focus more on my writing! You two are amazing and I am blessed to have you both in my life. Hope I don't make this weird by telling you both love ya!

To Louise, my editor and a tremendous supporter of my journey. Thank you for your editing skills and all the messages and memes you send my way. Love you.

To Becky, your proofreading skills are such a help with each of my books. I am blessed with your help and your friendship. Love you.

To my ARC readers, past and present, without your help and reviews, my books would be still unknown. You are all rock stars in my eyes. Love you all.

Thank you to my killer ARC team for this book. Cheyenne, Elizabeth, Amanda, Carina, Karen, Dakoda, Raven, Mandy, Lynn, Doreen, Debi, Marianna, Cassie, Kathy, Michelene, Ella, Sue, Stephanie, Scott, Liz, and Susan. Love you all!

Thank you to Bella Leigh Michaels, a fellow author, and Julie C., a reader, for your help in formulating the perfect blurb for this book.